SECOND-

Also by Sylvester Stein

Fiction

Old Letch
What the World Owes Me By Mary Bowes
The Bewilderness

Non-Fiction

Running for the Over 35s
99 Ways to Reach 100

Sylvester Stein

Second-Class Taxi

BRANDON

This paperback edition first published in 1990
by Brandon Book Publishers Ltd,
Dingle, Co. Kerry, Ireland.

First hardback edition published in 1958
by Faber and Faber Ltd.

British Library Cataloguing in Publication Data
Stein, Sylvester
Second-class taxi.
I. Title
823.914 [F]

ISBN 0-86322-117-3

Cover design by The Graphiconies (Ramaioli), Dublin
Printed by Guernsey Press, C.I.

CONTENTS

1

HOME BOY

Very early in the morning a large, heavily-patched army greatcoat wriggled and wormed itself along the inside of a wide concrete pipe until it was sticking quarter-way out into the frosted Transvaal air. Any military tailor present would immediately have set the coat down as dating from the Boer War. Even the patches on it had served an honourable lifetime, and had been pensioned off or patched in their turn. The coat lay quite still for a moment; then, having apparently satisfied itself that no one—not even a military tailor—was in fact present, it cautiously owned up to a head.

The head made further researches into the surroundings on its own account and confirmed the general satisfaction. It was a small head, covered with black wiry curls (known as peppercorns), and was connected internally in some way to two skinny, black hands, which now emerged from the sleeves of the large coat for the purpose of being blown upon and warmed up.

Then the coat shuffled right out of the piping and stood itself up on two cracked grey sandshoes, while the hands retired inside the long sleeves again. The whole object began to jump up and down inside the shoes for a minute, to generate more warmth, until it was encouraged to take the next step.

The head, in charge of operations now, arranged for the concrete pipe to be carefully slid back into the mound of assorted rubble from which it had been projecting like a gun-barrel from a pillbox. A broken-off motor-car door was pulled over the orifice of the pipe, and a cracked enamel basin plus a pair of aged kettles (one spoutless) were strewn around for the greater effect of casualness.

The large patchwork greatcoat—supported by the small head, hands, sandshoes and their above-mentioned internal connections—thereupon turned around and marched off in a military sort of way towards Johannesburg. But, as you were! It had seemingly left out part of its morning drill, for it immediately returned, to tug at a notice-board planted next to the mound until the sign, "DUMPING HERE" correctly faced the roadway. The march could now be resumed.

The tattered khaki greatcoat was the sole personal property of Staffnurse (commonly pronounced Stuffness) Phofolo, an African youth, the secret dugout at the end of the retractable concrete pipe was his sole personal residence—and the head, hands, connections, etc., also belonged to him. As the coat was four or five sizes too large for its inhabitant, it gave the appearance on the march of moving along on its own, a mere trace of black peppercorns visible over the top of the collar. At ground level the coat draped itself round the shoes. In the night, however, the coat turned out to be exactly the right size, for the hands and shoes were then able to retreat right inside it and keep away from the frost.

Staffnurse Phofolo was a vagrant, we are sorry to say. In terms of the law he was Idle and Undesirable, liable to instant arrest for having no Pass. If the law had known about his dug-out it would have become quite choleric, on the turn. For the rubble dump was situated within what was known as a European Area (though this was Africa). His very presence there was a threat to the delicate plant of European civilization; and the law, croaking apoplectically, would immediately have summoned all its forces to bundle him out of the place and direct him to Orlando Shelters. Orlando Shelters was an approved rubble-dump for Africans.

Unfortunately Shelters was full, the paraffin-tin shanties as well as the mud-and-sacking huts. Even the concrete pipes in the vicinity were inhabited to the brim. Staffnurse at least got his rent-free.

As to Staffnurse's Idleness, this was involuntary. He wished to work, not so much for its own sake as for the rewards it brought (four pounds ten a month); but as soon as he got employment the law picked him up and ordered him out of the Municipal area—because he had no Pass to seek work.

He thus would find himself out of work once more—and was then picked up for being Idle. Somehow he felt that the system was not running smoothly.

But he was a persistent character and this morning walked along to the nearest European houses (still on the continent of Africa, please) to find work once again. "I wonder, I wonder", he thought to himself as he trudged along. "I wonder if——" He couldn't quite recollect what it was he was wondering for the moment and went on thinking and humming in time with his march:

"I wonder, I wonder, I wonder,
"I wonder what I do wonder,
"I wonder what I gotto wonder,
"Boo-boom, boo-boom, boo-boom-boom."

He frowned hard to tear his thoughts back from the rhythm of his walk. "I *won*der," he thought, "I *won*der, I *won*der, I *won*der." He arched his shoulders upwards and scratched the back of his neck with his greatcoat collar. "Oh, yes, I wonder if I get a job today."

At the first house he came to he saw a white man in the garden, digging holes for three young trees.

Staffnurse stretched his neck out of the coat and over the top of the fence and grinned companionably at the white man.

"Job," he announced.

White man didn't say anything, didn't stop digging, didn't look round.

"Job," said Staffnurse again after a polite interval. "Gudden weck," he specified.

"Go away." White man didn't stop digging, didn't look round.

"Yes, baas," said Staffnurse, removing himself four inches along the fence and scratching his stiff hair humbly.

White man went on digging, went on not looking round.

After five minutes white man saw Staffnurse still standing there. He spun rapidly round to frighten him, waved his arms violently and shouted, "Go away, go away, go away."

Staffnurse took as much fright as caused him to move another two inches along the fence, then held up firmly.

"Want job," he said. "Fix gudden," he said, and pointed disapprovingly at the white man's digging operations. "She no good. I fix him," he added, treating his pronouns very casually.

"Go away, go away," cried white man in despair. He dug on but his haste caused him to cut his hand on the tin containing the first tree.

Two minutes later, seeing Staffnurse still planted patiently in the fence, he collapsed completely, said, "All right, all right, come back Saturday," and walked inside, sucking his hand. The trees were left in their tins and the digging was unfinished.

Staffnurse, having thanked the white man extensively, walked off to the city, while a tune relating to a "fat young Zulu lady all the way from Empangadi" hummed away in his interior.

He was passing along a busy road in the town centre when suddenly his buttoned-up nose got some information about baking operations in the vicinity. The nose emerged from its turret, took control and ordered a right-wheel into a confectioner's shop.

Here Staffnurse waited his turn while four European

customers who were there when he arrived were served. He then waited his turn again while another three European customers who had come in since he arrived were also served. After this the proprietor made an entry in a book, took a leisurely smack at a fly with his duster, and came round to offering the courtesies of his shop to Staffnurse. "Yes, Jimfish?"

Staffnurse pointed at a loaf of white bread and a bottle of green lemonade. "Him and him." He was handed the objects in a grand way, his elevenpence was taken (in an even grander way), and he then deferentially moved out of the shop to sit on the pavement, where he prised out the doughy insides of the bread and washed it down his throat with the green lemonade.

His face, now appearing from behind the coat, was seen to possess an enormous smile as its main topographical feature. The smile was planted out with large white teeth. Above it, for shade, rose a flat nose a trifle lighter in colour than the rest of the face. Threaded through the lobe of the right ear for decoration, as you or I might thread a thin gold ear-ring, was an empty reel of cotton (40 gauge).

His main article of clothing beneath his patched greatcoat was a torn, formerly white shirt, heavily patched to match and hanging outside his trousers in the fashion of the moment. These trousers were knee-length—on the average. That's to say the one trouser leg ended just above the knee and the other just below it.

Two furrows or paths divided his black peppercorn crop into four quadrants.

Staffnurse cheerfully cracked his smile wider open—to put his face in imminent danger of bisection, it seemed—and called over to an African delivery-man who happened to be cycling past, informing him of the fine job with excellent prospects he had just secured himself.

Staffnurse was no excessive talker, but he had to tell someone the news. The delivery-man right away put him in his place with a query about the salary the job would command. Staffnurse had forgotten to settle that!

"Hay, hay, hay," laughed the delivery-man raucously and expansively, and passed on this gem to the other Africans within hearing—which was to say all those within two or three blocks up and down the road (on account of the great strength and superior carrying-power of his voice). He found it necessary to dismount from his cycle and totter over to the pavement where he could enjoy the joke unhindered. "Hay, hay, hay, hay; ay, ay, ay," he howled, hanging feebly over the handlebars.

Staffnurse said nothing but laughed politely in accompaniment.

"Eh, eh," sighed an old African hawker sympathetically, as he trudged past Staffnurse, "It's a white man's world."

"It's a white man's world, uncle," agreed Staffnurse, his smile reduced to half power for the moment.

The smile soon returned to its job of absorbing bread and lemonade. Staffnurse had decided he was entitled to this blow-out, on the strength of the new job beginning on Saturday. It would anyway leave him a reserve shilling to deal with hunger problems in the two days that were to pass before then, and for the rest the future could take care of itself. The future had managed moderately well until now.

This impulsive, day-to-day philosophy had been forced on Staffnurse by his rather casual early upbringing. His birth was itself a casual affair, of which no more was known than that he was named by his mother, in African fashion, after the most important person at hand: on this occasion the white midwife at the charity African clinic where she arrived for her confinement after a seven-mile walk. The clinic, known as the African Clinic, being (as usual) full, she was discharged two hours after the birth, with a sixpence as rickshaw fare to take her home, and the blessings of the midwife to sustain her when she got there. She knew of better uses for her sixpence than wasting it on the luxury of private transport, and instead walked back the seven miles, the baby strapped to her back.

More than that Staffnurse didn't know. The question of paternity had often interested him, but beyond firmly maintaining his belief that there *was* some he could say nothing. He didn't know his date of birth, he didn't even know, as once his people did, his tribe. He was a frail infant, and survived two successive annual attacks of the Apricot Sickness only by two successive miracles. Once he could walk he followed his mother around at her place of work, two bandy legs supporting a brown potbelly and a runny nose. In summer, for form's sake, he wore an old vest rescued from the dustbin, almost long enough to come down over his navel. In the winter his wardrobe, coming from the same source, was a bit more extensive but quite as ragged. Generally he was neglected and ignored by the whole world, except by his mother, who gave him fierce soapy hugs when she could find a moment from her laundering.

At the Horse, Cattle and Native census of 194– he was actually left right out of the reckoning, due to official unobservance, so he not only looked like nothing on earth during his childhood, he was officially nobody on earth.

Hopes of being one of the lucky African children to get into a school therefore never arose. He quickly got a wide, varied experience in the "school of life" instead. At an estimated seven years of age he became a part-time carry-boy at the city vegetable market, his earnings several times exceeding ninepence a day. At nine he was enrolled in a European household as piccanin-in-chief. Here he blew the noses of the babies, shined the shoes of the older children, cleaned the master's car, swept the missis's floor, polished the stoep, attended to the boiler, did the silver, exercised the dog, washed the dishes—and got alternate Sunday afternoons off, at great inconvenience to the babies, children, master, missis and dog.

On the third of his Sunday afternoons off, he went to pay his usual visit to his mother, but she had vanished. He never discovered what had happened to her. From then on he was on his own.

At approximately thirteen he went down to Durban with the European family, who had been transferred. At fifteen they were transferred back again. At sixteen he was picked up by the police who judged him as being of working age and wanted his Pass.

Having no official identity, he had no Pass. To make amends for these omissions of his, he spent a week in gaol. On returning he found the European family had another piccanin in commission and were not going to take back someone "with a criminal record".

He had been playing this Cat and Mouse game with the police for a year or so now. In between he had earned enough to buy his second-hand greatcoat. The coat had already accompanied him to gaol more than once, so that it too had a criminal record long enough to set a magistrate shaking his head gravely. Now the pair of them would be "in" for juvenile delinquency, now for adult idleness. The law couldn't make up its mind. When "out" Staffnurse got himself jobs in a dozen different trades. He was a lift-boy, a house-boy again, a flat-boy, a cleaner in a barber's shop, and a sandpaper-boy in a furniture factory. He even picked up a bit of rough knowledge as tea-boy on a newspaper, though not enough to do anything for his pronouns.

He walked along now thinking with satisfaction of trying his hand at gardening. He believed that he might turn out to be quite an expert at it. Also it would give excellent cover from the police.

While he said this to himself, he saw a squad of police in their radio car cruising down the street, looking for business. As an immediate reflex action, he started to slip away along the pavement and jostled a portly white woman, who shrieked at coming into contact with this ragged black crow; then he panicked and broke into a run—and straightaway the whole street was in a furore. Two other white women began screaming, convinced that their handbags had been made off with, and the white men in the vicinity chased after him, determined to scotch this God-knows-what donder* of a kaffir. In Staffnurse's running and dartings between the crowd on the pavement, he started up at least half a dozen more Africans without Passes, two who were running illicit liquor, and one who was in possession of a "dangerous weapon", as defined by law. The white hue-and-cry caught one of them, and its racial appetite was satisfied. This one had been cornered in a basement shop and was frog-marched off, five white men holding on to him at once to show their part in the capture, and taken to the police, before whom he was charged with indecent assault, handbag-snatching, and possession of dangerous weapons (a pocket knife with two blades).

Witnesses came forward with names and addresses, including one elderly man who was certain he saw this very African not an hour before winking at a white girl and insisted that he be charged also with molesting her. This elderly man would like the crowd to notice that "they" were getting quite impossible these days.

Meanwhile Staffnurse had skidded round the corner, ducked into an arcade, stopped himself abruptly and slipped into a long queue of African office boys outside a sandwich supply depot. In front of him, gasping for breath after having performed the same acrobatic turn

* Donder (pronounced donner): literally, thunder—blackguard.

and scared almost coffee-coloured beneath his chocolate skin, was the delivery-man. He had also been caught up in the excitement, having a generally very frail conscience, The two of them moved up in the queue, which camouflaged them completely, until they came to the front. Staffnurse's last shilling went on a dainty postage-stamp sandwich filled with mock chicken mould, and he walked off with the delivery-man to help him find his cycle, which was abandoned at the start of the chase.

"These Europeans," said the delivery-man, shaking his head.

Staffnurse shook his head, too. The delivery-man looked around him carefully, then slipped a pamphlet into Staffnurse's hand, patted him on the back in a friendly way, remembered for a moment the circumstance of his not having arranged a salary, burst out laughing at it for exactly one second, patted him again consolingly and rode off on his business. But he was back again quickly, grabbed the pamphlet away from Staffnurse, read it through to him in one breath, and once more rode off.

Staffnurse turned the pamphlet around for a minute to get it into focus, and slowly repeated aloud the message he had just heard exhorting him to "Roll up" in his thousands the Saturday after next to show his support for the African Congress of Equality, and to hear a speech by the great leader, Induna.

He spent the rest of the day hanging around the delicatessen shops near the top of Eloff Street, admiring the kosher food in the windows, while he pulled out the pamphlet to look it over again. He found a passing African who could read, showed him the pamphlet, got it read over to him four or five times and repeated it back until he was word perfect. The two of them shook their heads seriously at one another. He found another African who could read and got him to read it out too, to check on the first man. Then he folded the pamphlet and put it carefully into a pocket of the greatcoat.

When it had become dark enough for safety Staffnurse walked home and retired for the night into his concrete pipe. Retired for the next day and night too as the most comfortable—and inexpensive—way of passing the time until he was required on duty.

Early on Saturday morning the greatcoat was again seen wriggling warily along the concrete pipe, shuffling out of the end, jumping up and down, and setting off for town. It was only just gone five o'clock, generally considered very early for a greatcoat to be out.

Staffnurse arrived at the white man's house and patiently queued outside the kitchen door until the white man almost knocked him down on his way out to work at nine o'clock.

With a groan the white man acknowledged Staffnurse's presence and put him on to digging holes for the three trees. Put him on to digging them good and deep, as a way of getting his own back.

"Oh yes, baas," said Staffnurse, knowing *all* about planting out trees.

He let the white man, Mr. R. F. Teep, go right off to work without having the courage to ask him the important question about what his rate of pay was to be.

But life was comfortable for Staffnurse at the Teeps'. Luxurious. He was allowed the run of a ten-by-eight feet concrete outhouse in the backyard and so was saved the daily hazard of making his way to and from his late hideout. He got a plate of mealie-meal three times a day (stiff and dry in the mornings, boiled up with gravy at noon, and made into a runny pudding in the evening), and occasional scraps from the white people's table.

Out of gratitude he dug the holes with great energy, until they were so deep there seemed to be some question of his having struck an outcrop of the main Johannesburg gold reef. He learned from the gardener next door how to fill in the rest of his time usefully and always gave a particularly fond watering to the three trees that won him his job.

At night he scanned his pamphlet by the light of a candle-end and turned in early.

By the time the Saturday after next came round Staffnurse was ready for the great meeting and "rolled up" at the open square, where it was to be held, two hours before the advertised time.

When it did get going—almost two hours *after* the advertised time—he was entranced by the new language he heard there, advising him to demand the vote, stand out for a living wage and "join our movement, fellow Africans". It was the use of the term "African" that affected him most. He was used to being called "Kaffir" (usually in the form "bleddy kaffir"), "Native," "Coon", or "Munt" often enough, and felt "African" a great improvement; quite distinguished enough to wear as a title behind his name—as, "S. Phofolo, African."

He had managed to trace the delivery-man in the large crowd. The delivery-man—Chops—greeted him with huge good fellowship, and winked and chuckled to remind him of his salary.

At every telling point in the speeches Chops gave him a nudge in the ribs as punctuation. On the platform—which was the back of a lorry—stood Saunders Xele, the secretary of the Congress; from the Cape, a fine well-built man, and a measured orator. He was a Xhosa and was speaking in Xhosa, waiting at every two sentences for the interpreters to translate his words into Sesuto for the benefit of his Basuto listeners, into Zulu for the benefit of his Zulu listeners, and into English for the benefit, it seemed, of the three white detectives sitting taking notes near the back of the crowd.

The detectives were quietly, silently, secretly reinforced by a posse of uniformed men who were using this convenient opportunity of catching a thousand Africans together to raid for passes. Before the raid got going Xele had reminded the crowd that the leader Induna would explain later that their congress movement was not directed against the whites. They—the Africans—were at any rate not racialists. This quiet, unranting stuff brought no nudge from Chops. Their job was to win equal rights for Africans. (A small nudge.) Not to take rights away from the Europeans. (Again ignored!) And he reminded them of the recent decision to boycott a certain baker's make of bread. (Series of enthusiastic thuds up and down Staffnurse's ribs.) Xele had hardly been followed on the platform by Boniface Zenze, who started on a more passionate note and suggested that the Africans were entitled to some of the good things of life as well as the vote—pure sedition, this—when Staffnurse got a beefier nudge than usual. He looked round politely: and found he was under arrest. The deliveryman had evaporated just in time, but Staffnurse was marched off in a crocodile with another forty of the audience. He craned his neck about to see the deliveryman, but all he noted was his cycle, temporarily abandoned again.

Staffnurse puzzled the police at the charge office by being able to produce no papers at all, not even a forged pass.

"Name, then," growled the policeman, a Constable Kees van Tonder.

"Stuffness Phofolo, baas."

"What race?"

"African," said Staffnurse, very pleased with himself at remembering to use this new designation, and hoping the policeman would be as pleased.

Constable van Tonder looked up aghast at this subversive nonsense, snapped "Non-European," and grunted that if he had his way he would put him down as a plain bleddy kaffir, and in fact would be inclined to greater accuracy by entering "bleddy Baboon". "Where from?"

"Non-Europe," said Staffnurse accommodatingly, wanting to correct the bad impression he had made.

Policeman, even more aghast, twisted Staffnurse's left ear, considered holding him for "disrespect to the uniform", and tried to squeeze out of it—the ear—information as to what kraal or location Staffnurse had originated at.

But there was no answer to that except a low "African Clinic." . . . terrible pause . . . "I mean 'Non-European Clinic'."

"Age?"

"Say seventeen."

Policeman wouldn't say seventeen, said eighteen.

"Previous convictions?"

Staffnurse on the whole believed not. Couldn't recollect any, anyhow.

Having got all these facts down on paper and impounded Staffnurse's pamphlet, the policeman came to the conclusion that he had here a really hardened Communist.

He dug out a stiffer charge than usual to bring against Staffnurse, who ended up with a four months' sentence as a farm labourer in the Eastern Transvaal, where he became acquainted with yet another trade, citrus farming (to the extent of being able to sew up orange bags).

During these months Staffnurse thought about the meeting and decided that he had heard there the sort of philosophy that appealed to him. He did not want to appear grasping but he felt that he might be entitled to something—if not schooling or the vote, at least a new greatcoat—by the time the Congress of Equality was able to bring in the millennium.

2

POTATO RACE

Staffnurse was released in the rural areas, temptingly near—or so the Law hoped—several prominent white farmers who were short of labour. The Law had thoughtfully left him unprovided with money at the end of his sentence so that he might be the more inclined to fall to the temptation.

But the cheerful fellow instead began the long trek back to Johannesburg, where gold and riches were to be found (in the form of £4 10s. 0d. a month) and where the offices of the African Congress of Equality were situated.

Staffnurse walked the first stretches, taking his sand-shoes off and hanging them round his neck by their laces for their better preservation.

He passed through the village of Waterval Onder, trudged up the pass from the lowveld, and reached Waterval Boven after two weeks. On he walked, in the dusty highveld. It was early summer now and there had been no rain to settle the soil for five months almost. When the winds blew up they carried half the soil over into the next province. The other half seemed, to Staffnurse's observations, to be collecting on him.

But at least the nights were warmer now. He sheltered a week in a friendly kraal by the roadside, earned a few potfuls of mealie-meal by helping to plough the five acres of land when the summer rains finally did come; and got tipped off not to pass near the district of Bethal, where the white potato farmers were so short of African labour (at £1 10s. 0d. a month) that they locked their farmhands up at night.

When he got on the road again Staffnurse made sure to skirt Bethal by at least twenty miles, and even then he walked along hiding deeper inside his coat than ever as an extra precaution, to avoid being taken for a possible recruit.

A big, grey panel-van came lumbering up from the west, nosed up to the bundle that was walking along, considered it closely, decided it was no sack of potatoes and stopped.

"Hey, you donder," called the white man at the wheel, "you want job?"

"Don't want job, baas."

"You want job, good money?"

"Don't want job, baas."

"You Rhodesian boy?"

"No, baas."

"You Portuguese boy?"

"No, baas."

"What kind boy you?"

"I non-European boy, baas."

"You donder," scowled the white man. "You cheek me, I arrest you."

"Yes, baas."

"Better you take good job instead."

"Don't want job, baas."

"What's matter, you loafer boy?"

"No, baas."

"You got Pass?"

"No, baas."

The white man's nose twitched, his eyes opened eagerly.

"Ho, you no got Pass, eh?"

"No, baas."

The white man turned to the two burly Africans next to him:

"All right, boys, sign him on."

The two men jumped out, grabbed Staffnurse and threw him into the back of the van—on top of several other sacks of potatoes.

"Donder," growled the one nastily, tipping him over with a toe.

An hour's drive—just enough perhaps to cover the distance to Bethal—and Staffnurse was thrown out of the van again.

"Go and fetch a hoe, you donder," shouted the white man.

"Yes, baas, where baas?"

"Don't give the baas cheek, you donder of a kaffir,"

shouted the African overseer, and kicked him hard towards the direction of the tool-shed. "Run, you donder, run."

Staffnurse ran, his shoes dangling round his neck.

"Now go and hoe, run," shouted the white man.

Staffnurse ran.

"Wait," screamed the white man, "Don't you want first fix up your pay, you donder of a fool." He rapped hard against his thighs with a length of rubber hose-piping.

Staffnurse ran back, panting.

The white man got out a ledger. "The pay here is One Pound Ten."

"Yes, baas."

"A month."

"Yes, baas."

"But you're new. I give you One Pound Five."

"Yes, baas."

"You get food free. Meat, too."

"Yes, baas."

"And your room."

"Yes, baas."

"But you pay two bob a month for uniform."

"Yes, baas."

"That leaves twenty-three bob," said the white man. "I charge you for your transport to come here. That's ten bob."

No reply.

"Yes?" shouted the African.

"Yes, baas," said Staffnurse.

"Leaves thirteen bob," said the white man, finally making an entry. "I pay you next month . . . breakages comes off."

"Yes, baas."

"Sign here. Make your mark."

Staffnurse made his mark.

"Now you work hard, you donder, or I'll fire you."

"Yes, baas."

"No cheek."

"No, baas."

"No reports to the inspector."

"No, baas."

"Run!"

Staffnurse ran.

The white man looked delighted. "No Pass, Zachariah; we've got him for good."

"Fine boy that, baas," said Zachariah.

"Fine material, Zachariah," said the white man rubbing his hands.

Staffnurse hoed all afternoon until he had blisters on his hands the size of the potatoes that would one day flourish here.

All round him the hoeing went on. There were young hoers, and aged hoers, big and little ones, none of them daring to let up for a moment, for fear of the length of rubber hose. Among that company Staffnurse and his greatcoat won all the prizes for smart tailoring. Some were in loincloths of rag, and the superior dressers were in sugar-bags, with holes cut for legs, arms and neck.

"Yes, it's the uniform," whispered Staffnurse's next door neighbour to him as they rolled over for the night in their concrete hutment, "Sugar-bags; unless you got your own clothes, then you don't get the bags."

"I get my two-bobs back if I don't use sugar-bags?" asked Staffnurse.

The neighbour sat up in his sacking-bed. "Kid, you get nothing back. But you'd never see that dough anyway. It all goes."

"Where to?" asked the kid.

"Deductions," said the neighbour airily, "Deductions he gives you every month."

Staffnurse thought he wasn't going to like this place. "Why you stay?" he asked.

"Dogs," said the neighbour. "Big ridgebacks. Besides I came from Nyasaland. Foreign Native. If I get out the police'll pick me anyway. That's why he catches us. You Foreign Native, too?"

"I non-European. Got no Pass."

"Oh, hell," said the neighbour.

The other men in the hut were all asleep by now.

"You heard of Congress of Quality?" asked Staffnurse quietly.

The neighbour had not. "Been here two years," he said. "What's that congress?"

"It's for voting," said Staffnurse, "and some new coats."

"Oh," said the neighbour.

"Can you write?"

"Some."

"You write for me?"

"Okay."

"Going to write letter to Congress, tell them about this man."

"Ha," said the neighbour unbelievingly, and fell asleep too.

Staffnurse's blisters grew bigger, smaller blisters grew on the big blisters, the small blisters popped, the big blisters popped—and still meat hadn't appeared on the menu. Still he couldn't get his neighbour to write a letter—"Don't even know address here," said the neighbour. Still they hadn't had an afternoon off.

Staffnurse thought the time had come to pull out of this unprofitable game of potato-farming.

"How?" asked the neighbour unbelievingly.

"In van," said Staffnurse cockily.

In the van they slept that night and were being driven away with a load of old potatoes before work started the next morning.

They crept out at a railway crossing and hid in the culvert at the side until the van was safely away. It vanished out of sight before the train's smoke had blown away.

Up poked a small field of peppercorns. "Huh," it said bitterly, looking the way the van had gone: "thirteen bobs."

"Deduction," said the neighbour, "deduction for transport away from farm."

The two set off along the country road. Staffnurse took

off his torn shirt and handed it over to his neighbour to wear over his sugar-sack. The greatcoat wrapped itself in compensation more tightly around its internal supports. Cotton reel swung in the breeze. Nose rested confidently on top button.

They got a lift on a donkey wagon between the next two towns and walked the last lap into Johannesburg in three days. As they arrived on the main road that crossed the outer suburbs Staffnurse was signalled by a fat white woman sitting at the wheel of a small car. "Jim, come here," she wheezed at him.

He obediently went over.

She pointed to the back of the car. "Push; car he break," she said, not doing Staffnurse's pronouns any good in the process.

Staffnurse pushed the car. "He" moved reluctantly forward for a few yards and broke into a fit of coughing when the woman threw it into gear. But still it would not start. "Push," she said sternly. Staffnurse pushed.

Another attack of mechanical coughing. Another push. A short coasting downhill, with cough after cough and lurch after lurch, when it was again persuaded to get started in gear. A push along the flat when it again wouldn't.

Staffnurse was joined by three jovial Africans from a road-mending gang—his neighbour was by now lost for ever. They got the car up to trotting speed and sent it whistling and wheezing and galloping consumptively as far as the next block.

Then their interest faded and they left Staffnurse to

carry on. He carried on and pushed until the car had arrived in home territory and coughed itself to a hacking stop outside its own front gate. The fat woman signalled Staffnurse to push it through the arch of jacaranda trees and over the asphalt path. It was laid up for a convalescent spell in its garage.

The woman got out, breathing heavily like a voiceless concertina, beckoned Staffnurse to follow her, and before he had recovered from his panting he found that he had been engaged as extra houseboy to Mrs. (Professor) Alida Hampshire, and had begun putting a high red polish on the front stoep. Of course, he had failed again to settle on his wage in advance.

Staffnurse had got himself into a liberal household. Professor Max Hampshire was a Member of Parliament well over towards the liberal wing of the Opposition Party. Liberality flowed over the household's domestic arrangements as well as through its politics. Every day of the week Staffnurse had meat, "boy's meat" as it was known, ordered from the butcher in a long list of cuts and joints that ended "... soup-meat, boy's meat, dog's meat."

Every week of the month he got an afternoon off, and every month of the year he got his £5 which was what Mrs. Hampshire had fixed on. Luxury indeed. Liberality indeed.

"Boy," said Professor Hampshire to Staffnurse when he first saw him, "Where are your white gloves? I don't wish you to be serving at table without gloves. Without white gloves. This is a liberal house but I do not wish its humanitarianism to interfere with the normal decencies. With the normal *human* decencies."

He pointed his finger across the dining-room table at Staffnurse. "You people will never achieve civilization until you've advanced from the tribe. Gloves at table, gloves for driving. Are you the new driver, boy?"

"No, musta."

"You have opportunity here, boy. There's nothing that's not open to you. Learn to drive and you in fact become driver. Opportunity. What's your name, boy?"

"Staffnurse, musta."

"No, your name, boy!" Professor Hampshire banged at him angrily. The professor could feel the adrenalin boiling through his heart and veins. "Not to let my temper juices run away out of control," he reprimanded himself silently. He stopped thinking, blanked out his mind, until the juices were slow and sweet again. He called up the staircase; "Lida what's this wretched ambulance driver's name?"

"Hampshire?" Her voice came windily down the stairs just ahead of her over-inflated person.

"My name Staffnurse, musta."

"Name does appear to be Staffnurse, Hampshire," she said sitting down to recover.

"Oh, impossible, ridiculous, my dear. What's your other name then, boy?"

"Phofolo, musta."

"Oh, damn, less possible still. The tribe—leave behind the tribe, we're living in a modern age. What was the last boy called, Alida?"

"Jackson," she wheezed in the upper register.

"Good. Jackson. You'll answer to the name Jackson."

"Okay, musta."

"And *I'll* not answer to the name master. I'm Professor Hampshire, not master Hampshire. You'll address me as Professor."

"Okay, baas Professor."

"Jackson, that word 'Okay' is no longer amusing as a colloquialism, and it's not yet correct as English; I would prefer yes if you please."

"Staffnurse," sounded Mrs. Hampshire, "You go sabenza work garden now. Turn finish hosepipe, push . . . push. . . ." She clawed for air. Out wheezed a few battered breaths while she held up a floury finger to keep him from leaving before she had got the rest of her instructions out. Slowly the concertina began to sound its full voice again; "Push lawnmower other side. Me want Ezra come here serve for table; tell him he come quickly."

Staffnurse stumbled down the back steps and escaped to the garden. "Ezra," he called, "She want quick," then started to dig up the potato patch, switching his thoughts to pleasant images of frosted bright-green ginger beer and small cakes with curly icing on top. "I wonder," he thought, "if ginger beer can come green."

"I'm not prepared to accept", said Professor Hampthire to his wife opposite him, "that one will advance one's principles a single jot by abandoning any of those principles. One must fight to keep the standards of normal decency all around one. Liberal in our politics, but conservative in our standards."

POTATO RACE

On Staffnurse's first afternoon off he took his coat off the hook and attended at the Congress offices. Here he joined up for a 6d. annual subscription (allowed him on credit) and hung around to get a glimpse of the great Induna, leader of the Congress, though now banned from belonging.

Induna came through, in spite of the ban, tousled the hair of the youngsters waiting around, gave Staffnurse's field of peppers its share of attention and walked through into the committee room.

A large smile broke out all round Staffnurse's face and the peppercorns shone in their pleasure. But he kept on waiting for something else.

Not a minute later and a new noise was heard in the room: "Hay, hay, hay, hay, hay, hay," it sang out—Chops, the delivery-man, just calling in for political inspiration and a supply of the new pamphlets, and laughing with delight at renewing the acquaintance interrupted by the police.

They went together to Chops's home in Sophiatown. He lived in a room in a small house in Toby Street, sharing the house with thirty-nine other people of all sorts and professions. In the house itself there were four families, plus a group of young men living in the room next to Chops. In the backyard of the house were the poorer classes, six more families in small home-made outhouses, each boasting large assortments of small children, as the lower-class families will do.

Most of these children seemed to be sitting at the door of Chops's room, waiting for him to return.

"We have a drink," said Chops to Staffnurse, after showing him his Congress membership card and a photograph of himself standing up holding on to the handlebars of his bike: "You have Scotch or Skokiaan?"

"No," said Staffnurse.

"Man, the Skokiaan is plenty strong," said Chops. "What then, beer?"

"No."

"Man, what you want?"

"Ginger beer."

"Ginger beer!" Chops was startled.

"Ginger beer!" The kids were startled too. Everyone knew where to buy Scotch, which was illegal, or Skokiaan, which was banned, but ginger beer. . . .

Chops sent the squad of kids scouring the area for a bottle of ginger beer. They dived into the drinking dens, the illicit bottle shops, the shebeens—but could come back with nothing better than an opened bottle of quite flat soda. This Staffnurse accepted and drank without murmuring.

"Music?" asked Chops.

The greatcoat nodded.

Chops kicked open the door and a worn recording of Duke Ellington's "Mood Indigo" came floating and moaning and scratching and growling through from the young men's room.

The young men, Africans, floated through too. The first one was a good-looking fellow, chewing gum and smiling secretly to himself. He was dressed in very smart, very narrow trousers, about twice as narrow as a respectable stovepipe, and a very smart, very wide jacket.

"That's Two Boy Sevenpence," Chops whispered to Staffnurse, giving him a nudge to impress him. "And that's Alfred the Great, and that's Alexander the Great." Two more sets of narrow-trousered wide-boys followed.

The three sat themselves down on Chops's bed, said nothing. Staffnurse said nothing, too, quite as effectively.

"Hay, hay, hay," laughed Chops weakly, a bit embarrassed by these great talkers, "Youse guys going out on the job again tonight?"

The guys said nothing, just closed their eyes to slits.

"Your record's stuck," said Chops next. It had been stuck for one and a half minutes.

"Back home, where de Dook comes from," said Two Boy Sevenpence, "we always stick it right there, see. Tzwee, tzwee, tzwee, tzwee; dat's de way dey like it back home in Harlem."

"Back home?" said Chops, "Oh, sure."

Nobody said anything further. The record went on: "Indig . . . indig . . . indig . . . indig . . . indig . . . indig. . . ." not tiring at all of the one phrase; the three young Africans went on chewing their sinister bits of gum.

"This Stuffness," said Chops, pointing at his guest.

The three young men looked at him slowly. "Yeah?" they said.

Staffnurse sat, the young men sat, the kids sat, and Chops now sat, too.

"Well," said Two Boy Sevenpence, getting up politely, "Guess we got to go now. Big job tonight." He pointed an imaginary gun: "Koyng, koyng, koyng, koyng, ker—plaink!"

They all three drifted out slowly, joggled the record on in their room and left the house.

"That's the leaders of the Torch Commando," said Chops to Staffnurse. "You heard of them, the biggest tsotsi-gang around here. They got terrific guns."

Staffnurse whistled. The kids whistled.

"Never do us no harm," said Chops.

They drained their drinks. Chops whittled a chip of biltong off a piece from his drawer, offered some to Staffnurse, gave the leavings to the kids.

They sat back. Staffnurse felt at home.

3

WHITE MAN'S WORLD

Government is a confusing thing at the best of times. The end of the parliamentary vacation in South Africa turns out to be not one of the best of times at all, for then the Government is preparing for a major upheaval.

Owing to an awkward historical precedent the Government has to spend half its year in Cape Town making the laws of the country, and the other half in Pretoria watching (rather anxiously) to see that the country carries them out. As Pretoria is one thousand miles over the veld from Cape Town, several hundred people, cabinet ministers, chief clerks and junior typists, who have to share their time between the two places, must undertake quite a journey twice a year.

So, just before Parliament was due to start its critical 195– season, all these officials and parliamentarians broke into confusion getting ready for the long train ride.

That's to say their normal settled confusion gave place

to a sort of galloping confusion, which rapidly spread its infection throughout the Body Politic.

What a bustle there was up at Government Buildings; hundreds of files being crammed into packing cases against possible use down at the Cape; all unfinished matters being hastily taken from the pending trays, scrutinized, heads scratched about them, and as hastily popped back into the pending trays ready for instantaneous "disposal" when the next vacation started six months later; surplus quantities of tea being brewed off at double strength before the departure; and earnest instructions being given to those clerks remaining behind to keep the avocado-pear plants in the window carefully watered.

What a bustle and confusion at the Prime Minister's official residence! And at that of the Minister of Railways. And of the Minister of Commercial Affairs, and the Minister of Industrial Affairs, and the Ministers of Finance, Defence, Interior, Exterior, and so on, down to the Ministers of Agriculture and Education and Arts; between them sharing out responsibility for the whole known world: animal, vegetable and mineral; spiritual, temporal and material; naval and military; land and sea; and not to mention profit and loss.

Only the Minister of Native Control, Meneer Kob, was calm in all this. He had shouldered aside his secretary and his private secretary and his secretary's private secretary, and done most of the packing of the files himself. This brief on native penetration into white areas had to go in, he knew, and that one on white penetration into native areas. He could not trust his secretaries to get things right!

A methodical man this, not in a hurry, yet all the time urging things onwards at a rather violent pace that reminded his critics, and even sometimes, with a shiver, his more astute followers, of Louis XIV and Metternich. He would have liked to cram every one of his 10,000,000 black wards into packing cases, too, if that were possible, to take them down to the Cape where he could keep an eye on them. But as the next best thing, he was planning a new law which he hoped would effectively take care of them for the next fifty years anyway.

A ruthless man this, yet who knew how much more ruthlessness he might meet.

Caught up in this commendable confusion of the white man's world was a young fellow who answered to the name of Jackson. Answered willingly and cheerfully, though no one had ever christened him with the name. Answered also to the name Staffnurse.

He was being taken down to Cape Town, too, riding at the back end of the trainload of political bustle and intrigue.

"Well, young domestic prisoner," a man was saying to him in the wooden compartment they were sharing with eight others down in the non-white portion of the train, "so they carting you along with them for their session, are they? How does it say in the advertisements 'Six-roomed house, linen, cutlery, servant.' A kind of a sort of portable piece of furniture."

Staffnurse smiled broadly, thinking it rather fine to be so portable.

"Prisoner," said the man, very brown complexioned, splendidly dressed in a thick sports jacket and highly-creased whipcords, "don't smile at such things."

Staffnurse laughed aloud.

Three other men in the compartment laughed, too, to keep him company. A fourth man offered him a pull from his Coca Cola bottle, to cheer him up. "There's more than Coca Cola there," he winked at him.

"The only way to accept imprisonment—is not to accept it," said the splendidly-dressed man. "You're in your cell, but you gotta fight to get out."

Staffnurse agreed just as cheerfully to this, so did the three laughers and the man with the Coca Cola bottle; only a fat, sad person in the corner shook his head. He shook it mournfully until his cheeks wobbled like a bushman's buttocks. He wouldn't have it that this was the sort of talk to give youngsters. "You'll lose him his job, mister," he told the man. His narrow eyes squinted out at the well-dressed man over the top of his cheeks. "Then there'll be another lad endorsed out of town. Your sort just gives the government more trouble, but nobody ever gains anything."

"Nobody ever loses anything," said the very well-dressed man, "because, really speaking, there's nothing to lose. But one day we're gonna all gain. Especially this Prisoner at the Bar over here. He's young."

"Look, Prisoner," he said to Staffnurse, "how's about me getting you to join up in the Quality?"

Staffnurse grinned, held up a finger to keep the man's attention, pulled his greatcoat down from the shelf he had stuffed it into, searched in its pocket and brought out his sixpenny-worth of membership of the Congress. He showed this to the man and passed a large wink round to the other eight passengers in triumph.

"Well," said the man, shaking his hand, "here's a bright-as-gold young fellow. Well, Prisoner, then we're on the same side."

"Yah, Mr. Zenze," said Staffnurse.

"Well, *Hell*," said Zenze, the splendidly-dressed man. "Hell now." He twined a springy curl round his finger and tugged it in amazement. "Hell, he saw through my incog."

The other men in the compartment buzzed among themselves when they realized they were sitting down with the famous Zenze, Wildest Flea of the Congress. All buzzed except the sad person, who sat mutely in his corner, sorry he'd ever interfered.

The man with the Coca Cola (and the little bit more than Coca Cola) dug around in his goods and found another bottle, which was passed around as further encouragement.

The train stopped at Kraaispoort. Zenze leaned out of the window into the heat, bought ten loaf-sized buns from a hawker and ten well-warmed Coca Colas (with nothing more than Coca Cola) and they settled down to get nourished while the train minced along on its long, narrow path again.

"I'm in surprised amazement, Mr. Zenze," said the man with the fortified Coca Cola, "that you should be on this train with us. Where is yours truly going to?"

Zenze looked at him a moment, head a bit askew, finger twirling his hair. Then he leaned forward, said to all of them in a whisper: "To release the prisoners!"

No one said a word.

Staffnurse looked around, glad they were all able to hear the big news with him.

The man with the Coca Cola finally got out his next question, in a careful whisper now too: "Which . . . which jail, sir?"

"Which jail?" replied Zenze, almost shouting now, "South Africa, sir, South Africa!"

Bottle of Coca Cola passed around swiftly for assistance while information is considered, checked for accuracy and digested.

"Ah," said the sad person with a fat sour smile, "the famous Mr. Flea is talking flea-talk here."

"If you would tell our good selves, sir," said the man with the Coca Cola, still inclined to be favourably disposed, "a little more particularly."

"Aw right," said Zenze, getting a good, thoughtful grip on his lock of hair, "particulars you'll get."

He cleared his throat to make it ready for the particulars, while the others gathered closer round him, except for the sad person who huddled farther into his corner though keeping one succulent pinky-brown ear well in circulation.

"Fellow prisoners," said Zenze as the train rocked its way between stations, "we've all got to break out together; otherwise, really speaking, we've got no chance of anybody getting out. Hey?"

No one said a word. "Hey?" he repeated.

"Yah," said Staffnurse quickly, as next most senior congress member present.

Coca Cola then nodded his head obligingly, and the three laughter men nodded sagely, too, allowing Zenze his point, for the sake of hypothesis.

"Aw right, again," said Zenze, marking them well up for this grasp of political science.

"But that's not all. No one else will help us. It's just us. Us and we alone. Yah, but not altogether alone—alone together. Getting together, sticking together, winning together.

"But *that's* not all."

The audience frowned, pursed its lips in its great learning and stood by for more.

"We've got to know what we're doing."

Coca Cola nodded slowly with enlightenment. Yes, yes, yes, of course. "Quite very necessary," he acknowledged.

"And it's the Congress that's going to help decide what. Really talking, there's no one else can do it." Pause for sinking-in.

"And now," said Zenze, "I'm going ask you to join our Congress of Equality, to help it grow and do the thinking." He took out membership forms from a wide inside pocket of his furry sports coat, handed half to Staffnurse and started enrolling the men. The sad person treated himself to a sneer and said that he had heard this sort of talk before, thank you, and he would hear it again, thank you very much, but no one was going to get sixpence from him. *If* you please.

No one did, but sixpences came out of old tobacco sacks, flashy wallets and frayed trouser pockets in large enough numbers.

"And now," said Zenze, as they rolled into their blankets that night, "I'll tell you this: get ready for the big boycott soon."

Staffnurse retreated into his greatcoat and felt ready enough right then.

Coca Cola sucked his bottle and decided it was a very snug secret he'd been told.

The fat person heaved himself on to the top flat bunk, let it take his weight and lay back heavily. The train rocked more wildly but carried on into the night.

We have done our thousand miles in the train; we have trundled respectfully past the goldfields of the Rand; hurtled through the straight flat miles of the karoo desert, creaked and croaked up the drought-stricken north side of the Hex River mountains, slid and skidded down their sodden south side, and we have reached the Cape itself which Sir Walter Raleigh called "The fayrest cape in all the world" (a phrase still remembered very warmly by the mayor, the councillors, the town clerk and the publicity bureau).

The M.P.s, by using influence—they proceeded without using influence only reluctantly—had installed themselves in seaside hotel rooms, convenient to bath and even more convenient to bar, where they proposed, as a matter of urgent importance, to get some of the colour back into their—noses.

The Hampshires, who answered an advertisement for a "seaside residence commanding position" were occupying it now and found that it commanded nothing much but a view of the subway under the railway line. It also commanded a high rent.

Settling in at the extreme rear of the seaside residence was Staffnurse, who managed the job quicker than anyone. He walked in, dumped his blanket and his cracked looking-glass, given to him by Mrs Hampshire, and he was ready for work. The only thing of value he and his greatcoat had now—was an identity. This identity, quite official, was ready to be sworn to at any time by an official brown pass-book which the greatcoat cared for in its securest pocket. The name the greatcoat now went under according to this pass-book was R. W. Mtetwa, aged eighteen, tribe Zulu, Mapok's Kraal. Staffnurse had been taken in hand by the imperious Mrs. Hampshire and his ownership of an identity was due to her great persistence, drive and energy, all used on the white officials in the pass-book bureau, in between rasping gasps of breath.

Staffnurse now kept his pass-book next to his heart, day and night, and found it almost as useful as the greatcoat itself in keeping the warmth in and the cold out. He still preferred his own unofficial name for normal, unofficial purposes, but kept Mtetwa for special police occasions.

Professor Hampshire had begun his planning of the first of a series of grand parties he intended throwing. He believed tremendously in what you could say to a fellow over a drink and still more to a lot of fellows over a lot of drinks.

The Ministers had moved out to their State houses, the Governor-General had arrived in the white train and all were settled in. The viceregal equipage had been taken around in a rehearsal of the official parliamentary opening ceremony, watched closely by seven cheering coloured youths, three retired policemen from the old people's home across the way, and three retiring squirrels (from an upside down position) in the oak trees in the Avenue. These thirteen stalwarts were back in their places a day later for the actual ceremony, joined this time by several score of other loyal citizens (who happened to be passing) and several other loyal squirrels (who happened to be hanging around).

Her Majesty's South African Parliament was open for business!

4

IN COCA COLA'S CLUTCH

Promotion in this white man's world, Staffnurse soon discovered, was rapid enough. He had earned his white gloves on arriving in Cape Town and begun to serve at table.

"Jackson," said Prof. Hampshire, in a benign moment, "I had assured you your prospects were excellent. Make certain of your fitness for the work. If you succeed in this you can almost definitely expect, also, an increment in your salary." The Professor turned to his wife, became petulant and said to her: "My dear girl, can we really have this native boy, though, serving at dinner when he persistently wears one of these tribal cotton reels in his ear?" Hampshire frowned. "And why just one ear!" he stormed, angered even more at the asymmetry than at the ornament itself. He could feel his evil juices bubbling away in his veins, but was powerless to stop them.

Staffnurse fingered his forty-gauge cotton reel, sticking through its hugely-enlarged hole in the one ear-lobe.

"Staffnurse," gasped Mrs. Hampshire placatingly, "take him out, this one no good, she catch too much plenty dirt that side."

Staffnurse stood perplexed a minute, scratched a wider path through his hair, then obediently tugged the cotton reel out of its hole.

"Oh!" Mrs. Hampshire's last breath left her in a little shriek of horror.

"Gracious heavens, no, no," shouted the Professor. "Replace it, boy, replace it."

A long, drooping loop of brown ear-lobe dangled slackly down where Staffnurse had taken out the reel. He put his finger through it and stirred around absently. Then he fitted the reel back, a bit uncertainly; stretching the ear taut again.

"Oh, really," Mrs. Hampshire puffed, as air escaped from her bagpipes. "Oh help me out, my dear," she implored the professor and waddled off with him, his lumpy nose leading the way doggedly, his ears standing straight out ready to come in for a landing on the stoep.

Staffnurse began his apprenticeship at table serving the Hampshires dining alone, or perhaps with their daughter, Andrée, who lectured at the University in Cape Town. For more formal meals he was smuggled out of the dining-room and put to cleaning the car.

"Mr. Mtetwa," said the lovely Andrée Hampshire to him one day as he was polishing, "did you ever go to school?" She was standing leaning through the car window looking sternly at him from the opposite side.

Staffnurse put down his cloth and looked around nervously. He felt sure he could be fired on the spot if someone was found calling him Mr. Mtetwa.

"No, missus," he said faintly. "Jackson, missus, Staffnurse, missus," he said, giving her the choice.

"Oh, dear, yes, we'd better preserve the master-servant relationship while we're here," she said with a tight laugh. "Well, Staffnurse, would you like to go to school?"

"My job, missus," he said, shaking his head.

"Oh, I mean after hours," she said, "say, at seven in the evenings."

"Job plenty time nine o'clock."

"Oh, but if we fix that, would you like to?"

"Yah, missus, too much," he said.

"We'll fix it."

Staffnurse was about to go up solo for the first time. The Coca Cola man had taken him through a course of driving lessons on the common at Green Point and was now serenely repeating his instructions to his pupil. "Don't frighten, fellow, I never ever gone and lost one single pedestrian yet, with my students. Patience, fellow. Don't worry for the pollismen and the traffic cops too much."

He sat beside Staffnurse, who was driving cautiously, bent into a hunch over the wheel, from the common through the one-way streets to the centre of town. The old canvas sign "Quick-Time Driving School" flapped at the back of Coca Cola's elephantine eight-seater Buick.

"It's of course much necessary you don't fright, boy," said Coca Cola. "Hey, use footclutch, you damnfool," he shouted at Staffnurse, as the car jerked up to a robot, "I tell you, of course, left footclutch before you brake."

Staffnurse and the Buick reared nervously at the shouting, Coca Cola howled again, Staffnurse stopped the car in half its length leaving Coca Cola's ears to go flapping forward with the motion and the back seat to crash on to the floor behind them. Coca Cola bellowed: "FOOTCLUTCH, not brake, you DAMNFOOL. You doan know how to clutch after eight damnfool lessons, you amazing damnfool." He pulled his pants up around his waist, tightened his teeth, and said to himself: "Patience, fellow, that's how we teach this driving art, by the way. Patience some more."

"Amazing," boiled Coca Cola away to himself as Staffnurse carried on through the traffic, "Mind you, amazing!"

"My method," he turned to Staffnurse to boast, "never ever got one pedestrian killed off. My method, that's still secret, boy, until you get your ticket. But my good self teaches 'em to drive solo quicker than anyone in this town."

"Dual Control College?" he laughed; "Money-back Motors?" he laughed again. "Doan make me laugh," he warned Staffnurse, "I send the boys on the streets after half that amount lessons."

"Now," he said, "Will yours truly turn up kindly into the Parade."

Staffnurse turned up kindly.

"My method stop students from braking too quick," Coca Cola said with a laugh that sounded megalomaniacal to Staffnurse.

Staffnurse threaded the dumb beast of the Buick between the buses at the terminus and through the second-hand stalls until he was on the Grand Parade square.

"Look, my frien'," said Coca Cola threateningly, pulling at the wheel to keep the Buick from rubbing its hide against an electric light pole, "Now you are going to learn quick. You first go across that way, my frien'. No doan hit these people, they going to catch their trains, there's nothing wrong for them doing that, eh? You say there's anything wrong for that?"

Staffnurse wouldn't say. He just kept his eye fixed straight ahead, picking and steering his way through the crowds rushing for the evening trains to the suburbs and the motorists driving away in their parked cars.

The huge Buick waltzed heavily over the crowded Parade. By the time he'd got near the other side a smile began to stretch itself again over Staffnurse's strained face. He was proud. A tuneful humming about a young lady in Zululand came from somewhere deep down in the greatcoat.

Coca Cola smiled also, in a sinister way. "You think you learning, my frien', you think you learned now?"

Staffnurse's broadest smile was answer.

"Well," said Coca Cola, "now come the proper thing. Turn back and cross over again."

The smile got whittled off Staffnurse's face . . . but soon returned.

"Now, I'm going to . . ." began Coca Cola—"DOAN hit that statue, you DAMNFOOL, it don't hit you back; NO DOAN REVVLE HER UP LIKE THAT". He switched off the engine and turned to Staffnurse when the car had lost steerage way: "Look, my frien', we got to do this again now when we get back to the beginning, you wasting my time. We got to watch for the pollismen and the traffic cops."

Staffnurse sucked his dry lips and made ready to turn her east a second time. The Buick also looked unhappy about this gauntlet running, its tappets chattered away, its lubricating oil flowed thinly in the heat and the gears began to clash.

"My method for stopping braking," said Coca Cola, "Is I switch 'em off. I disconnect you, my student friend, from the brakes. Yah." He snapped a link out of a wire on the floor near the driver's seat.

"No brakes now. Don't make no mistakes also."

Staffnurse looked at him terrified.

"DOAN LOOK HERE, LOOK WHERE YOU DRIVE MY FRIEN'."

Staffnurse looked back quickly, swerved around a traffic cop, and picked his way along at ten miles an hour.

"Now," said Coca Cola, "my ever-loving self jumps out and leaves you to swim alone, by the way. Good luck." He swung open his door on the passenger's side and vaulted out. "Keep going, of course," he called, "you on your own now boy. Mind the pollisman and the coffie traps."

Staffnurse steered for the edge of the Parade while

Coca Cola ran along behind him shouting. Staffnurse tried to stop her, couldn't make out how to do so without brakes. He tried to take his foot off the accelerator, but she started bucking again. Coca cola screamed at him from behind: "Revvle her up my friend, revvle her up," and off he went again, cantering through the crowds.

At the other end of the square he hadn't left enough room to turn around in, so had to make for the exit-way instead and shot through, into a stream of traffic on the road.

Then at last he discovered the mechanism of the clutch, and pushed it almost through the floor. The Buick floated to a stop right in the middle of the broad main road, while the rest of the traffic continued to flow past and around it in two streams. Staffnurse started thinking quickly about a heart-shaped swimming-bath full of ginger beer. Up came Coca Cola riding on the running-board of an elderly fruit lorry, to rescue him.

"That's it, boy," he was saying, "that's it, revvle her up and run. Never mind the pollisman. Amazing! very amazing work from yours truly. I can say, mind you, of course, I'm pleased with such amazing work from yourself."

Staffnurse tried to smile, failed, tried again, failed again, and said in a squeaky voice instead: "Okay."

"My method," said Coca Cola, "is quick-time, all right. I think you nearly ready to take off now."

Coca Cola clipped the patent Quick-Time brake link on again and drove Staffnurse home at tremendous speed—he'd been brought up in the no-brakes school himself. The Buick rattled where the bonnet didn't fit, rumbled where the spare tyre jumped about, tinkled where the number plates rubbed against the bumpers and jingled where the bumpers rubbed against the body. Rattle, rumble, tinkle, jingle, it went over the cobbled part of the main road; jingle, rattle, tinkle, rumble, it sang over the old tramlines, jubble, rinkle, takkle, ramble, it shouted gaily to the coloured youngsters up Constitution Street; they looked around to see what had dropped off the pachyderm worth salvaging.

Staffnurse sat cockily inside his greatcoat in the passenger's seat, winking at the coloured kids, and smartly saluting a white postman they passed, trudging up hill in his heavy grey uniform. "Yes, my sir," said Staffnurse.

The postman shook a furious fist at him.

"Oh," said Staffnurse sternly, "Oh, oh."

"You watch out, my friend," Coca Cola shouted at him above the rattling and rumbling, "I know these white guys, they do for you."

Coca Cola hummed along, over the new bridge and on to the mountain drive, until he'd come to Staffnurse's part of the world, and left him there.

5

DEMOCRACY IN ACTION

Three weeks later. Staffnurse had his wings. At the passing-out parade Coca Cola had congratulated him on being his youngest pupil ever and having gone solo in the shortest time. Staffnurse had learned to smile again and walked in to the testing-ground, pass-book in hand, able to face the traffic police without fear of being handed over to the government police.

Next morning Staffnurse, dressed in his house uniform of white calico ringed with red piping at the elbows and knees where it ended, shuffled up to Mrs. Hampshire who was sitting expanding and collapsing with each breath in her large grass chair, and presented her with his open pass-book.

"Now, what?" she said, churning around inside her chair towards him, "What, what, more pass trouble? Why you not stay here in your kyah, instead of running running all time town?" She snorted and blew. "Hey, hey?"

"No, missus, not pass." Staffnurse, politely handed her the book again, not pointing to the new insert, because it was not manners to point.

Inside she saw his driver's licence. "Oh," she gasped, "oh, Hampshire, oh, oh, here, oh."

Hampshire came running quickly from his study, where he had been busy at his Greek, taking his mind off politics. "What is it," he called, "my dear."

She couldn't answer, but thrust the book out at him.

"Jackson," he said sternly, giving his juices their head, and took the book. Then: "Gracious," he calmed down; the good juices began to flow, "is this you?" pointing at a vicious thumbnail photograph, of the kind used in convict records. It showed a scowling face, two narrow eyes and an earful of cotton-reel, all sticking up above the collar of an aged greatcoat, the whole captioned R. W. Mtetwa.

"Is me, baas professor," said the original of the face, with a large smile in place of the scowl, and two wide eyes for the narrow ones.

"Gracious," said the professor. Mrs. Hampshire was coughing and laughing at the same time, while she nodded excitedly, trying to say something also, apparently, but not able to get her message across through the other sound effects.

"Gracious, so you can drive, Jackson?" said the Professor.

"Drive fast, baas professor, amazing," said Staffnurse.

"Amazing, yes, amazing," Mrs. Hampshire managed to get out at last.

"Amazing," agreed the professor, "tremendous initiative and enterprise. Allow me to congratulate you for getting so far ahead of your environment. Ignore the call of the tribe, Jackson, advance with the new world; machines, money, morals, that's the creed to follow, not witchcraft and wishful thinking."

"Staffnurse," wheezed Mrs. Hampshire, "I think quick quick you make small rise, you too much clever."

Professor Hampshire frowned exaggeratedly at her from the other side of Staffnurse, shaking his head to contradict her suggestion. "Well, Staffnurse, we shall first see how you drive the Chev and later it will be time to think about any increment. You're young and there's a good deal of opportunity left for advancement, financially speaking. However, I think you can certainly accept our congratulations. Call for me at one forty-five at the front door, in the Chevrolet. All right you may go."

Staffnurse went.

"My dear Lida," said the professor, "How can you? Time enough surely to consider a rise when we do our annual staff salary reviews in August. We can't manage the extra pound at this time, my dear girl as you know, there's a devilish big tax to pay and the expenses of the move."

"Hampshire," said Mrs. Hampshire, "don't let me hear you argue again. Gets a rise end of the month."

Soon after one thirty the Chev was at the front door, shining and sparkling and looking in a holiday mood. Staffnurse jumped out of the driver's seat, went back for his yellow cloth, breathed on the door handle he'd used, polished it, then waited, standing at attention next to the back door, for Hampshire to arrive. Not an eyebrow of his flickered. Not an eyebrow of the Chev's.

"Jackson," said the professor, when they started off very slowly, "I think you're entitled to the information. I've changed my mind about that increment. I consider that any show of development like yours is to be encouraged by a suitable reward. You will receive a larger salary than usual as from the end of this month."

"Oh," said Staffnurse.

"To the House," said Hampshire, closing the subject, still faintly resenting his wife's forcefulness and his loss of face with Staffnurse.

At the House—two fifteen, and the division bells ringing for the afternoon sitting. By smooth, efficient timing, the ministers who had gone home for lunch all arrived in their official cars—shiny-black cars so long they seemed as if they would need tug-boats to help them when they berthed alongside the pavement. Staffnurse and his Chev jauntily threaded their way to the head of the queue.

"Hey, you donder," growled the white chauffeur of a ministerial Cadillac at him, "keep bleddy back."

"Yah, baas," Staffnurse smiled apologetically, pulled a lock of hair abjectly, nodded his head cringingly in agreement—and drove straight past. The Chev winked back at the Cadillac, full of brashness.

Hampshire got deposited in the House, told Staffnurse to be back at six, and greeted the ministers as they came in.

"Hear my speech?" asked Parpenfus, M.P., amiably as he padded past Hampshire in the Lobby, his legs appearing to move from below the knees only, in some remarkable way he had developed. It gave him a twinkling look below and an absolutely steady look above, as if he were riding a very small bicycle. "Hear my speech, hear my speech?" he wanted to know, interrupting a worried discussion between Hampshire and two other party men on the possible nature of the great (and terrible) Bill that Mnr. Kob had in store for Parliament.

"No, I am profoundly sorry, I did not, old chap," said Prof. Hampshire, turning to Parpenfus courteously, "I would have liked to very much."

Parpenfus did not stop but twinkled off brashly on his knee-high bicycle.

Hampshire became ferocious, the claws showed through the pads, he boiled up dangerous quantities of adrenalin. "The whips are putting that man up far too often," he snapped in his anger.

Before the currents in his veins had subsided Parpenfus was back—*he* was still as cheerful as ever, bringing a twinkle into the cold, marbled Lobby of Parliament itself. Parpenfus was a man who could not be put out of countenance. He was generally reputed to have a skin—or a hide, as it was put—as thick as a rhinoceros's. He was a short man, with short little legs (below as well as above the knees) but a very long neck, a still longer face, and running up and down it, the longest nose known south of the Zambesi River.

Parpenfus and Hampshire momentarily dropped their

inner furies and triumphs, to look with glassy eyes after Mevrou Hester Futsheim, the well-fed, bosomy wife of one of the up-country members. Their heads turned to follow her until the last curve of her mature profile swept through the side glass doors.

"Um," thought Hampshire. In spite of his intellectual city tastes he was fond of real country-bred gammon. "Um, a luncheon," his thoughts went on logically. The first idea of a politician at the start of a campaign. A political party marches on its stomach, as certainly as any other.

Hampshire's academic mind turned round and round on his political problem—it turned round until he was quite giddy and had to go inside the debating chamber to relax it. But it whirled round faster. He must make a bid for leadership of the liberal group in the party, the mind decided almost on its own. This proposition was subjected to minute analytical processes. The pros were set against the cons, and cancelled them all out, with a small spillover. This was weighed, tested for political properties, examined by sight and smell, exposed to the action of the air, and tapped to see if it was sound right through. Sound and accepted.

Off revolved the Professor's Mind again, at an even pace, working out how to carry on the new attack.

"A luncheon," it confirmed.

He saw his young supporter Levy coming towards him. Levy was a shy young man with a self-effacing way of walking right against the wall along the corridors while dragging his hand along the paint and humming absent-mindedly to himself—a throwback to his schooldays when he used to drag a stick along iron fences. Levy walked up excitedly and said, "I've been thinking up a luncheon."

Hampshire looked at him with measured lecture-room irony and a raised lecture-room eyebrow. "A remarkable demonstration of the power of mind over matter." Levy blushed badly, cursed himself for giving way to eagerness, while his hand nervously tapped the nearest stretch of wall for comfort.

But Hampshire agreed, he was captured by the luncheon idea (a demonstration of the power of matter over mind). He engaged Levy for that Tuesday.

The luncheon was half planned by the time Hampshire had taken two strides into the Lobby. Levy, Chipkin, his daugher Andrée, a freshly smoked snoek. . . .

Suddenly everyone cleared out of the Lobby. A bell had rung, strange Members had rushed down from the billiards saloon, out of the card-rooms, away from the three comfortable bars and through the swing doors into the House. Hampshire and Parpenfus joined the rush. The aged Pumpernickel had started out of a trance in the library where he had been improving his reputation for scholarship (though it is doubtful if he had been able to improve his actual scholarship, judging from his position of neck resting against chairback, mouth open and thin hands crossed against almost non-existent stomach). He shot through the doors just before the sergeant-at-arms flung closed the brass bar of the House and it was only by the neatest piece of judgment that he was saved from being bisected across his long slender frame there and then.

It was a division. A vote, as *you* might call it.

There was no one left in the Lobby, just a messenger flatfootedly carrying his tray of empty beer glasses across to the bar.

Ten minutes later the division was over, the Government had won by the usual majority of 93 to 59, the Opposition had breezily requested it to resign, the Government had just as breezily requested the Opposition to jolly well resign itself, and the members had returned to their billiards, their half-finished drinks and their critical hands of poker.

Hampshire pursued Chipkin to the door and invited him for Tuesday.

Pumpernickel quietly returned to the library for further study of the condition of the old Boer republics before the Boer War. He was quite a devil for study, his colleagues agreed. In fact this time he became so deeply immersed—in something—that when the bells went for the next division they did not rouse him, and his party voted one short. The billiards players and beer drinkers felt that the man was hardly pulling his weight.

6

THE GHOST CABINET

But what was afoot on this other side of Cape Town? What other debate of the nation was going on here, at Windermere Location? Who were the members of this conclave? What colour were its members?

They were black men. Oh, desperate characters, you'll say. Plotting, you may add. Inform Mnr. Kob, you may cry faintly. Isn't it the proper business of the white man to decide on the needs of the black man? If the blacks are debating something and have their own ideas about certain matters, it's plots and sedition they're busy with!

Without the benefit of Governors-General or of well-meaning squirrels, the ghost committee of the black shadow parliament of the country had started its sitting. Started it after a longish wait for late members, a longish pull at a largish jug of home-brewed beer for early members and an apparent determination by all members to keep discussing nothing that is on the agenda.

"My dear sirs," said the man with the longest pull, a young, sparkily-dressed, brown-complexioned fellow, "sirs, we gotto protest against this beer. Too weakish."

"Aaah," said an elderly gentleman in a soiled dog-collar, with an angry throat-clearing, "no, we must protest against this beer-drinking, and these Zenzes. They bound to spoil our meeting again."

"My friends," said the leader of the ghost cabinet of nine, "time we put away the beer and the quarrels. Can't going to see us skittling out this government on a diet of beer. Sammyboy, take it out."

Sammyboy sternly took out the jug, shoved it around the corner of the outside door and sat down disapprovingly again, on an upturned tomato box. Sammyboy, aged eleven, wasn't happy about the way the committee kept skidding right off its agenda. He took the world seriously and expected it to take itself seriously.

The shadow parliament hitched itself up and began to talk business, as a shadow parliament should do.

The nine men meeting here were working in the darkest secrecy. The names and identities of many of these leaders were secret even. True there was an annual public conference of their African Congress of Equality, but the presidents and chairmen and many of the members had been banned by the police long ago. As soon as new ones were elected to replace them, they were banned too.

Lately, however, the new ones had been nothing but figureheads. The police had comfortably gone on banning them, but they were just a "front" now, the real leaders were underground, so far underground that the police could not trace them, no matter how deep they dug or how far they struck into dark passages.

So, while the bannings and arrests went on at the surface, the real force of Congress was meeting and planning, oh yes, plotting, if you're going to call it that, in a shanty in the middle of the shantytown of Windermere.

Ho, desperate characters, you're right! No time here for beer and billiards, no nodding in the Library, no ogling in the Lobby.

When the beer got too busy, there was the shadow Reverend to vote for its removal, or Sammyboy, or the dour man in the corner who was in a hurry to *get* somewhere. This shadow cabinet member was the quietest, secretest of the men, even the nine hardly knew who he was or what he did. He said little, confided nothing, kept to himself. He had a woman, as dour and soured as himself—and that was all they knew.

There was that same cautious solid Xele of the platform, whose hut this was, whose son Sammyboy was. His passionate friend, Zenze, was the sparkily-clad swiller of the home brew. Xele was the link between the Congress's official and unofficial members.

And the leader, the huge, good-natured fellow, with the squattest of African noses and the fullest of African lips, hearty, bluff, common-sensible—it was Induna.

Here this shadow parliament was gathered in the black man's location at Windermere, where the walls of the shacks rotted in the rain, for they were made of sacking;

where the roofs tore off in the wind, for they were made of cardboard. The east wind blew bits of waste paper from the rubbish dumps of the city and piled them up against the long eastern fence-line until the wire fence was the backbone of a paper screen, more substantial than the shanty walls; the west wind blew hearty gorblimey stenches over from the sewerage outlets of the city, and laid them down in waves over the rows of shanties. In this middle part of Windermere Location, hardly a white man was ever seen at night, except a lonely lost sanitary inspector chasing after his errant clouds and vapours. Here the meeting was safe from plot-breakers.

The main business of the meeting was broached by Induna, who had an entanglement to clear up first between Zenze and Dube, a schoolteacher, about American-style shoes. The main business had to do with stepping up the recent boycott campaign until it became a real movement, not a haphazard experiment.

"The tests look good," said Induna, "no, they look really good. Strangely successful. For years the Africans have used the boycott—in its social, political, geographical, economical aspects. For the civilized African, it's our only weapon—otherwise there's nothing!"

"Nothing, nothing, nothing," agreed the Reverend. "There's nothing," he said, explaining it point by point to the others.

"The law will not allow us positive action, so we take a negative one," Induna went on, with a wink at the others over the Reverend's head. "We may not elect whom we like to our councils, because the government does not approve of this candidate or that one—then, we say, we will elect no one at all! While the vote still has got any meaning at all, and we have representative councillors or senators, then the boycott can be dangerous and wasteful and even self-damaging, even suicidal, even foolish. But our representatives today are there to state this man Kob's views, not ours. So we can safely boycott elections. We lose nothing. Nothing."

"Nothing, nothing," hammered the Reverend, after the nail was already well in.

"Yes, nothing, and that is boycott in its political aspects, isn't that understood, my friends?"

"Understood, agreed, accepted, passed nemo cono," breezed Zenze, "Least I hope this friend of mine Dube understands—when he doesn't tell me he understands how even to buy a shoe yet."

Dube pulled his schoolteacher's prim lips still more primly in and turned to the Reverend: "What does the Reverend gentleman think of this commonish American-style shoes?" he asked.

"Hê, what the Reverend guy thinks of American-style cant-gets isn't my cup of tea," said Zenze.

"We may not use the white man's buses to go to work," Induna went on smoothly, trampling over this talk of shoes, "well, then we will walk to work. This is geographical boycott," he said with a twinkle in his brown eyes.

"Nothing, nothing," the Reverend guy still muttered in his beard.

"We may not buy where we want to and what we want, or be served by who we want—well, then we won't buy! That is economical boycott," said Induna leaning forward, earnestly and angrily now. "That is economical boycott, my friends! That is it!"

The meeting growled its understanding, agreement and acceptance of this too.

"This economical aspect is new and it is powerful. Powerful." Induna roared the word strongly. "It will be *negative* action with *positive* results. For years there was nothing we could do in this economical way. *Nothing!*"

The meeting automatically turned to the Reverend to hear his responses. He felt his dignity was hurt and grumpily stayed silent.

"Our economical influence was too small," said Induna, "When a man got thirty shillings a month, he couldn't keep back much of that from the market without starving. His mealies, his shilling meat he must have.

"But now people have begun to earn £10, £20, even a few millionaires we have produced at £50 a month, and people have begun experimenting. In one town they decided—no one knows where the command came from, but it grew among the people—they decided to boycott a tea-room."

"Yah," said Zenze, "and in Grahamstown they cut off those butchers, hey? Cut 'em off sharp, boy."

"In a third town they decided to boycott bakers."

Sammyboy sat with his fists clenched, remembering.

"The boycotts had no very ambitious goal, you can remind yourselves, my friends," said Induna, "the tea-room was boycotted to teach the owner to respect the importance of a queue. He learned quickly to respect the importance of the African's spending power—and the other thing followed."

"Hah," said Zenze with pleasure, punching Dube hard on the arm in a cordial sort of way.

"The butchers were being boycotted because they cheated the Africans. They gave the worst cuts for the highest price, they counted out the wrong change—if a man complained he was hurried on, pushed along—and they turned the Africans right away if there was a shortage.

"The boycott moved forward to a new phase when the bakers were attacked. This was to win a right, not simply to correct a wrong. And it was one of our branches that directed the people in this."

The meeting stirred aggressively.

"The bakers would not employ African workmen. They were proud of this, 'Only European labour used', their labels said. Yet they sold their bread and cakes and biscuits to Africans and all. There was no label to say 'Only European customers'. Well, these labels of theirs were quietly left off.

"In these boycotts we could see a new economic force show its strength. It had plenty of strength to show, my friends. After exactly one day. . . ." Induna held up one big index finger and showed it around to the eight men, with a great deal of delighted emphasis, ". . . after one day the tea-room in the first town had agreed that well of course it was wrong to keep Africans waiting in the queues, and well of course first come must be first served, which they said was an excellent business principle, oh yes, quite excellent, and well of course the people must understand they valued the Native custom as much as the European."

"That was not nothing," said the reverend with a chuckle. The rest of the meeting relaxed and chuckled too. Sammyboy frowned less severely.

"The Naytiff trade is the backbone of my business," quoted Zenze.

They laughed again.

"The recording industry in this country, shareholders should observe, depends on the urban Bantu," mimicked another shadow minister, "the Bantu have a wonderful feeling for music, gentlemen, it's something born in them."

They laughed louder.

"Hey," shouted Zenze across the narrow room, "you ever heard the whites singing that Skokiaan?" He got off his paraffin-tin chair and started capering around the room, singing, "a-bingo, bingo, bingo, bing. Happy, happy, happy, Africa."

Two more joined him on the floor, laughing and clapping, stamping and swaying, until Induna called them to order. Sammyboy had looked away embarrassedly.

"To Business, sirs! After a day or two," said Induna, "some of the butchers and the bakers found that just the same sound business principles applied in their trades too. But some of these tradesmen, in their apartheid bull-headedness, would not give in for quite a while.

Their business fell away, and especially those right inside the location suffered.

"The boycotts were quite a success."

Induna had come to the end of his first chapter. He cleared his throat, looked around, tickled Sammyboy behind the ear—drawing a very serious smile—and began again.

"Then the Africans went a little further. The Congress stepped in. Saunders Xele stepped in to run a little campaign. He called for the spitfire boycott against a fruit trader in a Location, demanding that the trader refer to Africans as Africans and not Natives. The trader, this little immigrant from Greece, Mr. Paul Panapopolous" (the meeting in spite of its anti-racial principles couldn't help allowing a little smile to smirk across its face) "did not know what it was all about and just wanted to be left alone to make enough money to go back to Greece—this was a man very sensitive to business principles," said Induna with a twinkle, "and he soon came round.

"Then the Africans went further. Too far, in fact, and our friend Xele had to lead them back. One Location, very pleased with its successes, called a boycott against a shop because it would not keep the European customers waiting until all Africans had been served! And another group of young workers thought it might be a profitable idea to boycott the local gaol, because it served inferior food to African convicts. But our sensible Xele made a lightning dash to their headquarters and talked them out of it. He explained to them the value of going to a plan. Then this group was all for *not* boycotting the gaol and actually offering themselves for arrest, to show their goodwill towards planning in general and to admit how wrong they had been. But Xele talked them out of this too.

"The boycotts have shown the power of money and they've shown how even the poor can wield that power. The boycotts have been successful up to now, without public propaganda or picketing—just by word of mouth and example, which is very sure."

"And very safe," grinned Zenze.

"And very safe. But these have all been simple boycotts. Now, my friends. . . ."

The friends listened twice as earnestly.

"Now the party must be ready to work on a big plan, a plan prepared these last few weeks by Xele and myself.

"First! Where can we hit hardest? I will tell you. Where we have just and moral demands. Where we spend most of our money. Where we can afford to boycott without doing ourselves damage."

The meeting recognized the great logic of these conditions.

"If we pick on a boycott of mealie-meal, for instance, or of bread—we might as well be embarking on a hunger-strike."

The meeting recognized this too. "Quite," said Dube, "quite, quite, quite."

"We must choose our targets very carefully."

Recognized again.

"Well, the time is nearly here for business—for trying out our own 'sound business principles' . . ." out came the twinkle once more, ". . . and we must soon tackle the boycott on a mass socio-politico-economic scale."

The meeting held its breath in concentration. Sammy-boy was a statue.

"Our aim is eventually to threaten the major industries and producers of the country if they do not recognize our just demands. Eventually!" He cautioned them. "As we told our friends who went too far too fast, we must work to a plan.

"Now, which industry shall we strike at first?"

"Now, what about cigarettes," the impecunious parson, the Rev. Nkomo, put in eagerly. He could not resist a useful side-swipe at the devil, while getting in one at the mere earthly oppressors of the people.

"Yah," shouted Zenze, who, though on reasonable speaking terms with the devil, wanted action soon, on anything.

Induna shone an innocent smile around and rubbed his hands. He said that he thought not yet, but cigarettes might be considered later, certainly. He took out his twinkle, breathed on it and polished it up brightly, before letting go an enormous wink at Xele. No need to tell the Reverend that cigarettes was in fact one of their own suggestions in committee. Cigarettes were made partly by African labour, but the Africans complained that in certain factories they were not given "important" enough work. They made the tea for the other workers, swept away the tobacco dust and drove the lorries. Yet in other industries they were also given packing and machine jobs—at higher pay.

The requests for better work, said Induna, would be tied up in complicated trade union demands. If not met, the cigarette manufacturers would learn by diplomatic hints that a boycott threatened. If they didn't come round the boycott was to spread through the country, backed by the Congress.

Jam-canning was another suitable manufacture. If improved work and wages were not offered—the Africans would switch their brands, even go without jam if necessary.

Newspapers next. "We want to be referred to as we want to be," said Induna. "We will see how long they hold out when we stop buying."

"Very true, very logical," said Zenze.

Induna held up an oversize hand, like a policeman.

"But these boycotts are not to begin yet just awhile."

Zenze did not see that *this* was very logical, and frowned severely, as though logic was his strong point. He twirled a curl of his hair absent-mindedly around his finger.

Induna explained how necessary it was for the boycotters to get more practice yet, to try their muscles on simple struggles, to wait until they commanded a watertight case. If they were successful in a few elementary boycotts, the mere threat of one later might be enough to win their points. "And after all it is winning our various principles that we are out for—not fighting a boycott war."

Zenze wondered at this, twirled his hair rebelliously at the thought that he might be done out of his boycott war, then broke into a rapid laugh as the justice of the argument finally found its way through to him.

"We must triumph our principles," said the Reverend.

Well, Induna acknowledged, they had to make a start, a small start, in a countrywide way. He proposed extending the original quarrel about queues to all shops, as the first thing.

Zenze seconded this so quickly you'd think it was his own idea, and there was a tendency for everyone else to add their names to the resolution somewhere. Accepted!

The meeting relaxed and sat back on its upturned paraffin tins, its empty tomato boxes and its one kitchen chair. Zenze put a cautious arm outside for the beer jug, and took a cautious swig. They began discussing the workaday details of the plan. Even Sammyboy permitted himself to swing his legs over the edge of the table, as an acknowledgment that the serious business was over.

Jackson, the dour one, prowled away into the night by himself—he was not one to be afraid of the location robbers and tsotsies. Indeed they showed all the signs of being afraid of him.

A rather sharper wave than usual drifting over from the sewerage dump, the rest of the meeting broke up and wandered off into the dark location after him. Xele and Sammyboy replaced the paraffin tins beneath their bed and curled up in it head-to-toe.

7

SHADY LADY

The gentle old Rev. Nkomo walked out of the hut with Zenze. He thanked him warmly for backing up his cigarettes suggestion. There was an odd fellowship between these two.

He gave Zenze a reproving a little shake of his head, sighed, was about to say something, but could not get it out, and sighed again instead. Zenze sighed too, to keep him company, twirled a lock of his hair round his middle finger thoughtfully: "Sadie, is it, the Rev. Nkomo?"

The Reverend walked ahead and said nothing, so distinctly it was quite clear his problem was his daughter, Sadie. He walked on with more reproving shakes of his head at Zenze, and with sorry nods of his head at himself at finding this final confirmation of the wickedness of the world—which of course he had always suspected.

They hadn't gone more than a few paces into the middle of the Location when he gripped Zenze above the elbow and huddled to a frightened stop. A shape detached itself from the dark wall of the next hut. It was a large shape, a very shabby shape—a very tattered Army greatcoat mysteriously being moved along towards them by some insubstantial agency in its interior.

"No," said Zenze with a great laugh, "no, the Rev. Nkomo, don't worry, this is my young friend Stuffness."

A row of white teeth shone through the darkness at Nkomo and Zenze from inside the coat as Staffnurse Phofolo signalled his delight at being introduced.

Induna caught them up now, and Staffnurse was presented to him also. He ruffled the peppercorn head and chuckled loudly in the darkness; "Oh, yes, the famous non-European from non-Europe. We have heard of you, young fellow." He delightedly rubbed his huge hand over Staffnurse's head until each individual curl was stinging sharply, and slapped him on the back until he staggered.

Then Induna turned serious, clasped Staffnurse around the shoulders and told him: "You insist on your rights as a human being, my lad, and you will help Congress and your people. Don't let anyone call you kaffir—and even more important don't you let them treat you like a kaffir. Teach that to all your young friends, and to your old friends too!"

Induna strode off. Staffnurse fell into step with Zenze while the Rev. Nkomo continued to shake his head at Zenze. Again he sighed and said, "It is Sadie. Yes, it is her, my son. Do you learn any more of her?"

"Well, no, my Reverend," said Zenze, trying to fit discouragement, reassurance and helpfulness all into one combined look. The look turned out to be something of a failure, lop-sided, and mysterious. He twined the twist of hair round and round his finger at a great rate to cover up. "But that girl can't be far away, of course. I will still nevertheless look," he said.

Zenze had put the discouragement into his look because he knew Sadie, the Reverend's runaway daughter. Knew she would not be doing anything that could please her old father. But he mixed in the reassurance and the helpfulness because of his kindly heart, which hated to disappoint people or to tell them unpleasant things—even if true.

"Oh, you needn't worry about that girl," he said, now working himself up to believe that everything was going to be all right. "No, she'll be fine." He gave another look now, this time trying to convey just the helpfulness and reassurance, and no discouragement, having quite talked himself around.

He hadn't talked the father around, though, and the Reverend sent a mild, disappointed, frowning look at him, as if to say it was just his jolly, eager type of character that had made the world wicked in the first place. It would not be surprised, the frown seemed to add suspiciously, if it had a good deal to do with the circumstances of Sadie's particular wickedness.

Zenze and his lieutenant, Staffnurse, escorted the Reverend Nkomo home to his own part of the Location, then carried on through the night, which was so beautiful above, where the same stars shone down on black and white alike, obeying—to the annoyance of the government!—no apartheid principles, but which was so sinister and ugly below.

Zenze marched on through the squalid huts with a rather blank look on his handsome, brown face, and steadily twirled his lock of hair to see if any useful ideas might be induced to appear through that channel. The method seemed to work, his face brightened up, he changed his course and started to swing over to the town side away from the direction of the wind with its particular offerings. Staffnurse swung along with him.

They walked along the broken streets—to give the Location ditches their full title—and arrived at tarred, lighted roads which began at the boundary of the European area. Zenze here negotiated a Police patrol, showing the policemen who leaned out of their black Ford squad-car a certificate that proved he had been working as a plumber's boy in Maitland, Cape Town, and made no mention at all of Port Elizabeth, from which city he had in fact just returned from organizing the last small boycott. He also brought out a "night special" signed by the same non-existent plumber, giving him permission to be out after curfew time for Africans, and finally he showed them his Poll Tax Receipt and his Location Permit. Just to be friendly he offered them a glance at a photograph of his wife, a strapping beaded Zulu woman (also, though, non-existent) standing with four naked children, and allowed certain pleasantries to be made about her. He received the leg-pull with great slappings of his buttocks, and talked to the police in the bucolic clicks and clacks of their home language, Xhosa. He did not intend showing them that he spoke English quite as well as they did, so marking himself down as an "educated cheeky boy", immediately. He put on such a convincing act that one of the African constables confided to him that they were out looking for the Communists and agitators of the Congress.

Zenze recovered his papers and walked on more quickly now, to get to the Congress offices in the Langa Location, where he could warn the top men that the police were "out" tonight. A certain well-known greatcoat once again attached itself to him, after it had spent a period in the shadows, through a lack of eagerness to meet the police patrol. Zenze swung off down the street, loping in that typical veld-lope of the African that disposes of the miles without any effort, until he got to Langa. Meanwhile the greatcoat was sent ahead to the other side of Windermere on the quest for Sadie.

The lack of eagerness on the part of the greatcoat to entertain the police was a reflex action now, coming about through long training, though no longer necessary since the birth of Mr. Mtetwa, late of Mapok's kraal.

This Mr. Mtetwa had decided to appoint himself personal aide-de-camp to Zenze, the African Flea, the Man whose Words Bite. Thereafter he had spent his spare time following the Flea about whenever he was in town. Zenze was temporarily "working up" the Cape Districts, where he proposed to take a particularly hard nip at the arm of the law.

Following Zenze's instructions Staffnurse stepped along towards the farther part of Windermere on the trail of the wilful, wayward Sadie. He poked his head inside a corner shack he had been told to watch for. It was a shanty shop, which carried the sign, "Out of Hand Sales Conducted Daily Ask for Prop W. Twitch." Inside this shack were five adults and what must have been about nine children, judging from the quantity of legs and arms that were involved in some junior kind of African Battle of Waterloo. Staffnurse respectfully addressed the oldest adult, an African with a stubble field of grey hair sprouting over his head and asked if he happened to know anything of Sadie Nkomo who lived here last year. This question caused a sharpish-looking woman sitting next to the grey-haired man to bridle immediately, and it was quite clear that she did know something. The sharpish-looking woman had a sharpish-sounding tongue and indicated that this something that she knew wasn't entirely to her liking, either. "Oh," she said, throwing her head towards the ceiling, "Sadie Nkomo!" However, the aged African, prop W. Twitch in person, politely told Staffnurse that Sadie had lived here until quite recently, when, owing to a surprise visit (he coughed tactfully here as a sign that one could guess who Sadie would be getting this type of visit from) she had disappeared for a while and returned to a different part of the township, later.

"Three months, as a fact," he said, also now looking up towards the ceiling.

Staffnurse politely looked up to the ceiling also. "Does the uncle know where she's gone exactly now?" he asked with great tribal respectfulness and indirectness.

The uncle didn't know, but thought that in the next street at her place of business (another tactful cough) they might know.

Meanwhile the riders and the donkeys had disentangled themselves from their Battle of Waterloo, and going on the fact that they mustered sixteen legs (and precisely the same number of arms) Staffnurse estimated that there were eight children in the room. The oldest was a pretty girl of about fifteen. They had all been watching with great, open-mouthed, open-eyed interest, throughout the conversation, and the excellent timing of their giggles showed that they knew at least as much about Sadie as did the sharpish woman.

Staffnurse thanked the grey head and didn't forget to throw in a polite smile to the sharpish woman, the other adults and the eight children. Off he went down the street.

Off down the street, too, went an escort of the eight children who were going to point out to him just where the next street was in case he couldn't find it.

The place was shut, but next door there was a very old twisted African lady, with a very old twisted nickel-plated teaspoon dangling as an ornament round her neck, sitting on a step and smoking a mealie-cob pipe. The aroma seemed to show that she was burning some home-made tobacco—and home-made of dried paw-paw leaves the aroma further showed. It caused her to spit frequently for relief.

"Does the grandmother know where Miss Sadie Nkomo is?"

"Never seen her," (stream of tobacco juice).

"Sadie Nkomo?"

"Who?"

"Never seen who?"

"Who you speaking about?" (another stream).

"Who I speaking about?" asked Staffnurse, muddled.

"Sadie Nkomo," said the smoker, supplying her own answer.

"Where has she gone?"—Staffnurse tried again.

"Gone." (Positive water spout.)

"Where?"

"Away"—pointing vaguely all round.

"Does the grandmother know where anyone can find Miss Nkomo," Staffnurse went on, quite heartened at the information he was getting out of her.

The grandmother spat carefully at the bottom step, just next to Staffnurse's foot and let out an acrid cough of smoke just next to his nose.

"Perhaps the grandmother could tell me where she is?"

"Who?"

"Sadie Nkomo. Perhaps the grandmother could tell me where she is living?"

Perhaps the grandmother could, but the grandmother preferred to let fly a hugely contemptuous round of spits instead. She kept her pipe out of her mouth for one carefully enunciated phrase: "Never heard of such a woman." Pipe replaced.

"Isn't it true that she works in this very house next door, if the grandmother will just think a bit."

This called for a stream of indignant spitting that rattled off the corrugated iron like hail, together with a short denial of any knowledge of Sadie Nkomo and an announcement that there was no desire to pass any such knowledge, if it did exist, to any agent of the government that might be asking.

"But the grandmother is wrong, because it is the father of Sadie Nkomo, the Reverend Nkomo, who wants to know."

The spitting let up. A crafty look replaced it. "The Reverend Jolop Nkomo?"

"No, my grandmother, the Reverend Josiah Nkomo."

"Ah."

"Yes, my grandmother."

"The Reverend Nkomo from Congress?"

"Yes."

The spitting started again but with a new friendly note to it. "Then why didn't the young man say so, instead of pretending he was from the police." The pipe prodded him for an answer. "No the young man is wrong."

A last delighted shower of paw-paw leaf juice came from the old woman who then and there confessed that there was nothing she would like to do so much, of course, as help any member of the Congress, and of course she knew Sadie Nkomo. But would she have told a police spy? she asked with a momentary return to her anger. She knew exactly where the young fellow could find her. Her place of business was moved again, to number 1021 Fourteenth Street. Pipe returned to mouth, old woman returned behind smoke screen.

Staffnurse and his escort, now grown to twelve, moved off to Fourteenth Street. There he shooed them away and they reluctantly returned to the old grizzle head and the sharpish woman, to resume their Battle of Waterloo game in the exact position they had reached at Staffnurse's entrance, the four new recruits being divided out between the opposite sides.

Staffnurse knocked quietly on the door and out came a handsome finely-built young African woman, dressed carelessly, so that she was almost tumbling out of her thin print dress. This was clearly Sadie Nkomo, Staffnurse decided. Behind her in the passage was a tall African, dressed in a Basuto blanket, strumming a guitar like a troubadour.

"Well, man!" said Sadie after studying him for a moment.

"Well, man," echoed the troubadour vaguely.

Staffnurse explained his mission. Sadie welcomed him generously, led him past a dozen earnest drinkers to an inner room, asked how her father was, blew a kiss at the idea of a visit from Zenze, and poured a tinful of kaffir-beer (nicely topped up with hot brandy) for Staffnurse. He quietly sucked it down, realizing at last that this was a shebeen and Sadie was the queen hereabouts. He realized also now what caused her to change her place of business so frequently—the law, which does not allow Africans to drink hard liquor, not so much on moral grounds, for white morals are allowed to suffer in this respect, as in further honour of the glorious principle of apartheid.

Staffnurse then walked out again through the same drinkers, seriously getting on with their business, and went off to direct Zenze to the address.

8

GOD IS A REINDEER

Tuesday. Lunch at the Hampshires. Cape sherry, lobster thermidor (known down-town as baked crayfish), a fat slice of oily smoked snoek, milk-fed chicken, Cape hock, pancakes in rum, fruit in a basket and a liqueur glass of spicy Cape Van Der Hum.

There had been a careful selection of guests for political purposes; a weeding-out of the liberal-minded from the simple-minded, as Professor Hampshire put it. And there had been a careful reinforcement of the table staff to place the sherry, lobster, chicken and so on before the select guests.

Staffnurse had been seconded from his driving duties —after a hurried sweep through the suburbs in the Chevrolet to bring in carless guests—and had his gloves of office on again. Staffnurse was nervous, though not as much so as Levy, M.P., who was clinging to the side of his chair and humming under his breath to keep up his spirits. Mrs. Hampshire, after a day's canvassing of

Coloured voters, whom she had positively *ordered* to "put in" the liberal candidate for the town council, was now positively *commanding* Eloff, Chipkin and two very pale young ladies to admit that they had *never*, at *any* time, even *tasted* as fresh a snoek as this, admit it now, ad*mit* it!

The two pale young ladies, dressed in blue organdie, also very pale, were somebody's daughters. The guests had not quite remembered after the introductions whose daughters they were, but it was taken as a practical hypothesis, to be accepted generally, that they *were* somebody's daughters.

The young ladies had pale views, to match the pallor of their faces and their dresses very nicely. They were liberals, but they let it be known that they were not going to be *extreme* about the matter, and they held that the Natives should be allowed to feel their way only very, very slowly and very, very gradually. The feeling and the gradualness are indicated by holding up the right hand in a pinched gesture that might easily be misinterpreted—by ill-intentioned people—as meaning Stop!

The elder of the young ladies (and neither was so very young, it has to be confessed), saw Staffnurse come into the room and leaned over to explain in disguised terms: "Of course there would be chaos if progress was not measured. You would have People who did not know their Places; People who would demand our Places and I fear many People who would no longer agree to fill the necessary, essential Places."

Staffnurse passed the Worcester Sauce to Chipkin,

M.P., at his request, and saw him shower it over his milk-fed chicken, turning the bird quite sour, then add some of the specially concocted sauce and a quantity of gravy. Chipkin sopped his bread into the three sauces and stirred them all together, while Staffnurse hurried back to the kitchen to tell the chef the horrifying thing that was going on.

"I won't support such a Bill whatever the Party decides," Chipkin was saying to Andrée Hampshire. "It's not a good Bill, it's not a necessary Bill, it's. . . ."

"Nationalism, sectionalism, sensationalism," said a cultured voice digging into the conversation from the opposite end of the table: Professor Hampshire putting in an approving word for Chipkin's statement. "Chipkin, if the Party decides on collaboration with the Government on this Bill, then Hampshire fights on as an independent. Hampshire joins the maquis."

Levy cheered this nervously, the young ladies said nothing but clearly were not maquis-minded and Andrée tossed her pretty head rather, to show some doubt in the strength of the resistance movement.

Chipkin picked a grape off the bunch dangling from the handle of the fruit basket, sloshed it in the sauce and sucked it absently. Staffnurse snatched away his plate before he could repeat the blasphemy.

By the end of the pancakes the first reading of the Bill had been outvoted, by the fruit course the second reading had taken a nasty fall and by the Van Der Hum and brandy the whole thing had been totally discharged, rejected and thrown out.

GOD IS A REINDEER

Four o'clock. The guests were gone; Staffnurse was padding past out of the dining-room for the last time in clearing away the dishes when the professor spotted him.

"Jackson", the professor called to him, "a word with you!—on a matter not connected with business."

"Yes, baas professor."

"In this Parliament of ours there is a measure due for introduction, shortly to be brought in by that Minister who is responsible for the care of your people. I do not approve of this Minister and I do not approve of the measure he will propose, one that will give him complete power to rule your people on his own, with very little consultation among the rest of the body of voters."

"Baas professor," said Staffnurse intelligently. "Boo-boom, boo-boom-boom," he imitated the professor's rhythm beneath his breath.

"I think you should know that neither Mrs. Hampshire nor myself is ready to support such a Minotaur of a Bill and that we intend to fight it bitterly. We expect in this matter support and encouragement from you and your people, on whose behalf we are in fact acting."

"Yes, baas professor," he said earnestly.

Hampshire sat leaning back in his chair, thinking for a moment or two, then sighed aloud. "Do you believe in God, Jackson?" he asked.

Staffnurse scratched his skull slowly in reply, ready to fall in with any of the professor's wishes.

"Do you believe that God exists as a stern, aged bearded man with a trident in his hand?"

Staffnurse fingered his cotton-reel ear-ring thoughtfully.

"No," the professor assured him, of course he didn't accept such an obsolete sentiment. Then in what form did he believe God existed?

"Wait," commanded the professor, peremptorily holding up a hand to forestall any reply. "As a genial, aged bearded man with a team of reindeer? No. As an avuncular, aged bearded man with a number of stars and stripes on his hat? No, Jackson, you don't believe that in this modern world. As an aged woman, perhaps? a legendary She? No, though why not, what is essentially masculine about the concept of godhead, I demand?

"Perhaps, then, finally, as one of the very reindeer? No, the thing is not to be conceived. Can Man have any clearer conception of any God there may be than a fish has of the nature of the water it swims in or of the man that hooks it? To the fish the god Man is a long, thin piece of cord with Danger on its end. An awful God. No, even if there were a God—and I don't want to state anything here that may shake your own fundamental faith—if there were, Man would not know of his existence and could not grasp it.

"So, Jackson, what is there for us to acknowledge? What else is there, man? What else?"

"Bass professor?"

"I will tell you. There is only agnosticism. A learned admission of ignorance. Humble appreciation that we know nothing, feel nothing, have faith in nothing, that we can neither confirm nor deny the fact of God;

yet, as cautious scientists, adding perhaps, that our inclination, feeling and belief is against the existence of any mystic, superhuman, supernatural, superstitious, moral agency."

The professor sat and sighed again. There was silence. He turned round. He waved his hand at Staffnurse. "You may go."

Staffnurse made a dash for it. The professor sat quietly for a moment or two, then sighed again. "A thin piece of cord," he repeated to himself. He belched politely. How many slices of snoek, he wondered amiably, could dance on the point of a needle.

In the kitchen Staffnurse gave a report on the after-dinner conversation to the chef. "That professor drink too much brandy."

9

RADIO-INACTIVITY

It was the day the famous Horror-Bill was to come out. Professor Hampshire was to go in early in the morning for once, to prepare for it. "This is the H-Bill, Jackson," he said on the drive in. "It can explode the whole of our world if mishandled. A nuclear legislative monstrosity."

The professor hummed to himself. "But you can rely on us of the maquis, my boy," he said, patting him on the knee confidentially, "to fight it. To fight it to the death," he pronounced dramatically.

"An H-Bill. A progressive reaction, but not representing progress. A reaction, certainly representing reaction."

Staffnurse dropped him at the House, then dropped the car at a garage for an inspection and, the day ahead of him, made his way to Langa to see Zenze.

"Ko-ko-ko," he called, knocking on the door in the Location fashion, imitating the sound of knuckle on wood. "Ko-ko-ko—can I come?"

"Ko-ko, ko-ko, my boy," called a delighted voice from inside.

Staffnurse was given a mug of beer to store away inside himself. "Prisoner," said Zenze while they were sitting facing one another, "we got a fight on this afternoon with a Hell-Bill."

Staffnurse reached automatically for the comfort of his cotton-reel, his face dropping rather.

"I've elected you to go to Parliament with me today," said Zenze grandly.

"Been already," said Staffnurse.

"Been?" Zenze snorted. "It isn't no joke, you prisoner of sorrow, I don't joke over such trivial affairs."

They went out into the sun and made for the suburban railway station. They queued up at the ticket office, inside which a clerk, Old Short Change, was dispensing the railway tickets, levying his private tax and nodding away sleepily. The ticket clerk kept back a few pence of the money tendered by each person. If anyone complained that he was entitled to more change, the man growled at him, waved him away and barked furiously: "Move along, move along, or I'll call the police." People were scared to "cause trouble" and did not report him. The old residents simply took care to bring the exact amounts. Yet he still tricked some, depositing their tax in a little wooden box marked Staff Subscriptions and laughing to himself weirdly.

Staffnurse stood in the queue just behind Zenze. Zenze produced a half-crown, with a flourish, for his elevenpenny Location return. The man handed him the ticket—without looking up—plus a bare one-and-three-pence change from the till. Zenze twirled his hair, did some estimating, tapped on the counter and coughed. Still without looking up from his papers the man felt for the remaining fourpence in the till, and dropped it in the Staff Box.

Zenze twirled again, estimated again, tapped on the counter, and said in the plummiest of voices, a special baboo act of his, "Now on this question of my change, good sir."

The good sir looked up, narrowed his eyes and growled. Zenze went on unperturbed, slapping himself on the chest. "You've got an educated African here, you cannot cheat him like those ignorant blanket Bantu, good sir."

The man began to jab his pencil in the air at Zenze, shriek and create a tumult. Zenze leaned against the wall, and tapped blandly on the hollowed-out wooden money-counter. "I have my very rights, of course." The fuming in front of him went on, the queue behind him shoved and fussed, but Zenze insisted on his very rights.

Finally, when the clerk noticed out of the side of his eyes that the train was pulling out and the whole queue had missed it, he grudgingly threw the correct change at the "educated man".

Staffnurse came to the window next and offered a shilling for his elevenpenny ticket. The crazy clerk winked at him: "An educated man is one who knows how many 'e's there are in elevenpence," he said. He gave Staff-nurse his penny change, as a gesture of confidence, leaned closer to the hole in the window and breathed secretively into his ear: "Five."

"And", he called after Staffnurse, "how many there are in elevenpence ha'penny." He cackled hoarsely and shook his box at the queue.

Staffnurse felt that there was something profound and illuminating in all this, available only to those with schooling, and that it was no doubt the main key to the mysteries of the white man's world.

Zenze and Staffnurse jounced into town on the train, walked up to the House and asked if there was room for them in the public galleries. Room there was for non-whites, the man allowed, though he was keeping back a long crocodile of whites. "In the first bay," he told them.

Zenze walked briskly upstairs and along the corridor, Staffnurse hurrying to keep up with him and asked in a worried voice: "In the bay?"

They were shown into the one tiny seating bay kept aside for non-whites. Even their arrival did not fill it, though the rest of the bays and galleries were overflowing with whites waiting for the Bill to come out.

And in seven seconds the Bill was out. Mnr. Kob laconically proclaimed it to the House and the keyed-up galleries, and set down the start of the debate for eight days' time. Then the next item on the order of business was on.

Out rushed M.P.s to the Lobby, leaving a quorum to keep the business going. The public in the galleries, who didn't know that everything important was over for the afternoon, waited behind for whatever it was that was supposed to happen, to start happening. All that did happen was a learned engagement on company tax among the polite quorum of Members.

The public pointed out the Prime Minister to each other—there were four distinct and different identifications, all equally wrong—and then the public frowned hard trying to make out from its knowledge of parliamentary procedure what time the H-Bill was going to "come up". The public concentrated hard, but its knowledge of procedure was limited. The public fidgeted in its seat, the public cleaned its finger nails with the corners of its train tickets, the public counted the number of M.P.s with hearing aids, then counted the number with beards, then counted the number on each side of the House and considered it extremely unfair that the Government should have more than the opposition. The public began to fidget even more and leaned over the side of the gallery and bays to see whether *any*thing was going to happen until the ushers tapped it on the shoulder and reprimanded it for disturbance. The public sat up straight, very embarrassed. If this was *all* that was going to happen today, thought the public, then, *really* it didn't *know*. It couldn't understand what all the fuss was about.

Pumpernickel, the Oldest Member, came out of a short doze, executed with his eyes open, a trick learned to fool the Speaker, and surfaced into the company tax debate. He, like the public, was puzzled as to the fuss about a mere fiscal measure; stumbled out of the chamber and off to the library pretty clear in his mind that at his age and experience it wasn't much use getting excited over day to day crises. "And what if they do declare the undistributed dividend as taxable in certain classes of private companies . . ." he asked himself irritably.

The public could hardly put the matter better itself and gradually sauntered out of the gallery. Other members of the public who had been queueing up all this time to get into the big debate, excitedly took their vacant places and settled down to wait for the dramatic fight on the Horror Bill. This new public fidgeted, cleaned its nails, counted the hearing aids, the beards, leaned over the side, etc. . . . Only in the small non-white bay was there empty space.

"Well, that's Parliament for you," said Zenze with a lordly flourish as they marched away down the street, "that's what we're fighting to have a say in."

"H'mm," said Staffnurse, paying a careful amount of attention to the partings in his hair.

"H'mm, I wonder," thought Staffnurse to himself, as they trudged along, "I wonder, I wonder," he sang underneath his breath in time with their steps.

> *Parlee*ment, *Parlee*ment,
> *Fat white* la*dy and gently*gent,
> *I wonder*, *I wondering* . . .
> *Boo-boom*, *boo-boombering*. . . .

His thoughts wandered off until he ended with a silent sigh. "I wonder if Parliament can get me coat?"

Zenze walked along with Staffnurse who went to see if

the Hampshire car was ready. It was. Zenze climbed in beside him and grandly waited to be driven away.

Staffnurse looked at him in a worried way.

"Quite all right, my boy," said Zenze, "I'm going back to the House myself."

Staffnurse still looked worried. He shook his head. "Professor's car," he said.

"What?" Zenze looked at him horrified, "and can't a Congressman drive in it? We all got to stay prisoners for always? What's this professor done?"

Staffnurse put the car in gear and slowly, still a bit worriedly, let her move forward.

He set Zenze off just before they got to Parliament, received a bow for his trouble and went to park the car until the Members came out.

10

HOW MANY BEANS MAKE FIVE?

Here is that Boer War greatcoat out walking at night once more. It seems to have a great deal of business to transact after the regular hours. If it does not take care—and keep in close touch with its legal representative—it will find itself "in" again after its long spell "out". What mission is it on this time? What message does it carry to what dangerous conspirators?

Up it climbed along the High Level Road, to a rich-looking house on the moonless side of Table Mountain. It mounted the slippery red steps, crossed the slippery red stoep, went up to the front door—the front door! an African!—and rattled the knocker up and down, but very gently.

A young European woman, with fresh, lightly-spun hair the colour of apricots, came to the door. She looked at the caller a moment, gave him a quiet smile and pushed the door wide open.

"You're Staffnurse," she informed him, pointing at the middle of the greatcoat.

Staffnurse cautiously agreed on this item.

"Yes, you're the non-European from non-Europe," she told him, her quiet smile turning into a quiet laugh. He sidled timidly inside, taking up as little space in the passage as possible. "Well, never mind," said the young woman, giving him a comforting prod in the middle of the coat, "I suppose, in that case, I'm the non-African from non-Africa."

Staffnurse felt that this admission quite evened things up. The young woman shook his hand—his hand, please note—and told him that she was pleased to meet him. Staffnurse replied that he was pleased she was pleased to meet him. The door closed.

Here was sedition for you, if you like. When white and black begin to mix, anything may come of it. The young woman with the apricot hair should have been warned. Front doors and hobnobbing! Time enough for a Bill to be brought up.

Inside the house Staffnurse followed the young woman. He was still so intent on effacing himself that he retired deeper into the greatcoat than ever before. Even the topknot of peppercorns sank modestly out of sight below its plimsoll line.

He was led into a little room. While he was kept waiting a moment, he shyly rubbed the palms of his hands up and down his flanks. Then he was seated at a low drawing-room table, and given a pencil and empty book, which he was required to fill up.

When he worked up the nerve, he looked around and saw that there were eight other adult Africans sitting about at tiny tables and at children's dainty desks, also busily filling in little books. At least, seven of them were; the eighth was apparently busier frowning at the effort of academic thought—and picking his nose absent-mindedly, as an aid to that effort.

This was education. Yes, a short step to seditious practices; agreed! It was the Tuesday night elementary class at the free night-school run by Mrs. Lennon. Staffnurse was the newest boy at the school, sent there by Mrs. Hampshire's daughter, Andrée, to have his pronouns sorted out. The boy who never went to school had quite fixed his mind on getting an education. Congress talk, always noisily going on about education, had convinced Staffnurse that it was something romantically desirable.

What had really impressed him, also, about the value of education, was Zenze's success with the railway ticket clerk. It gave him a great respect for education and determined him to discover whatever possible about the "five eezz" in elevenpence.

"Tables, ladies and gentlemen," said Mrs. Lennon. "The twice first."

She turned to Staffnurse. "We're going over our twice times tables first, Mr. Staffnurse. You no doubt know them?"

Staffnurse nodded guiltily, feeling he was expected to have some basis in something.

"Right," she said, "in that case kindly just follow with the rest of the class."

Staffnurse followed—a table or two behind—and intoned "twize two in four, twize three in six." He soon felt he had the tune perfectly and began to embroider harmonies around it: "twize two 'n six, twize three 'n six, twize four 'n six boo-boom-bi-boom." Staffnurse felt he was getting near the root of the money matters that had puzzled him on the station. Excitedly he went on, hoping for a revelation about five-eezs soon.

"Stop, stop, stop," Mrs. Lennon rapped just a little testily on her table. "I believe there is someone who doesn't quite get the hang of these tables."

No one said anything. She turned to Staffnurse: "It's not our friend from non-Europe, is it, perhaps?"

Staffnurse shook his head confidently. He was certain he was not letting down the choir.

"Would you perhaps let us hear you on your own, young man," said the lady with the apricot hair.

Why not, thought Staffnurse and gave her a full bar or two of the lesson. He couldn't quite remember the words and hummed it instead.

Sniggers came from the class, particularly from a houseboy who had that week carried home a certificate awarded him "For Outstanding Scholastic Achievement —First in Class."

"Maybe you could explain to our new friend," said the apricot lady to the Scholar.

"Sure, sure, sure," he beamed at her. "Son," he said to Staffnurse, "This is times tables. If you have one only one time, that's one, hey?"

"Ahuh," said Staffnurse.

"And if you have two one time, that's two, hey?"

"Ahuh."

"And if you have one two times?"

Staffnurse's hand moved uneasily towards his skull, scratched it awhile, but nothing emerged.

"It's two also! son," said the old scholar, patiently. "Now my boy, if you have two two times—look first here's one two on this desk, then I can put another one two next to it. Right?"

"Yah."

"Right, then, easy, how much is that?"

"Oh," said Staffnurse, catching the game, "Two and two in four." He smiled excitedly around.

"Excellent, young man," said the teacher, clapping, "but please remember to say two and two *is* four, I think that's where your mistake was. Now that's what we call *twice*—two times."

"And three times?" asked Staffnurse.

"Trice," said the Scholar.

"Three times is trice, and four times?"

The Scholar opened his mouth, coughed once, said doubtfully: "Four times, you ask?"

"Yah."

The scholar looked at the teacher who replied briskly, "Four times."

"Three times is trice, but four times is four times," said Staffnurse disappointedly. He didn't see much chance of success with five at this rate, the magic seemed to run out so easily.

"Today we're just on the twice times," said the teacher firmly, and they went on with the song.

By the time the first lesson was over, Staffnurse had a still greater respect for education, but he believed he now knew most of the import of "five eezz" having met e shortly after his formal introduction to a, b, c and d.

He found himself a confident enough member of the world by now also to give Mrs. Lennon a cheery good-bye on man-to-man terms, then left the house, again by the front door, whistling about "that Zulu lady of mine" and in between humming thoughtfully to himself that two and two was four.

The determined Miss Hampshire said to Mrs. Lennon: "Fine material, that," and seemed to be mentally measuring him out at so much a yard.

Mrs. Lennon agreed: "He'll learn quickly." Miss Hampshire nodded her lovely head darkly, but she was not thinking of *that* kind of material, or *that* kind of learning; pronouns and prepositions were not all to her.

Staffnurse's singing soon tailed off as he got into the Main Road. He confided the news to his greatcoat that, if Mnr. Kob's Bill was passed, their new school might become illegal.

The greatcoat considered Staffnurse's information for a minute or two but made no comment. Staffnurse himself sighed at the thought of being parted from education—this new-found friend of his.

He was making for Windermere again and passed the public swimming bath on his way. It was after swimming hours but someone had left the front gate open and Staffnurse walked in, sat on the benches round the side, wondered what it'd be like full of dark green ginger beer, and tried out the spring in the diving-board, just to see how it felt to be in a grand white-only swimming bath. He was considerably liberated on the instant at this triumph over the colour bar and marched off again with some of the diving-board spring in his own step.

He had enough of it left when he came to the next police patrol to wave cheerfully at the cops instead of ducking down a side street. "Baas, too mush plenty cheeky-boy there she's frighten ladies," he told the white sergeant and his tall corporal, picking out his choicest pronouns for the occasion.

He pointed precisely down the street to the corner where this grave, though completely imaginary, incident was taking place. He watched, still more cheerfully, as the sergeant and his men climbed aboard their Government Ford and squealed down the street on two or three of their tyres to save white civilization. Then he smartly loped along, in the opposite direction, to be sure that the sergeant wouldn't find another cheeky-boy (in a torn greatcoat) as a substitute when he came back.

Staffnurse ducked under the Location barbed-wire just at the point where the smell from the crayfish-canning factory met and mingled with the smell from the great sewerage works, and walked on between the shacks until he reached Sadie's shebeen. There was Zenze, in the middle of a beery debate on the H-Bill. Some of its clauses had got themselves blown up rather larger than life-size by now, and the proposed opposition to them was taking the same sort of shape.

"No, man, we'll go leave for Rhodesia," said Liquorice Boy Kekana, the man with the guitar, firmly. He knew a way across the Limpopo and was himself quite prepared to lead the ten million Africans into this land of milk, honey and freedom. Kekana had in fact crossed over into Rhodesia this way before, though he seemed to have forgotten that there he worked for two pounds ten a month and was kept very severely "in his place". Wasn't much of a place, either, he might have remembered.

"Hey, if you only knew what's in this Bill," sighed Zenze, turning to Staffnurse. Staffnurse did know most of it, but didn't want to spoil Zenze's story, so he listened politely to a clause-by-clause commentary.

"One: ethnic marriage," says Zenze. "Stric'ly Zulu to Zulu, Tswana to Tswana."

"Well, we can get married in Rhodesia," said Liquorice Boy morally. Somehow he had managed *not* to get married to at least six females in his own country in the past few years, law or no law, shotgun or no shotgun.

"Two: ban on gatherings. Not more than three people together."

"Yah, soccer, boxing, jive sessions, banned also." Liquorice Boy threw in a bit of invention.

"Three: no town businesses."

——"Whites'll take 'em over."

"Four: No private education."

——"Nothing private at all."

"Nothing!" said Staffnurse, "and night schools?"

"Private night schools, private day schools, private nursery schools, private mission schools, private correspondence schools—all must be closed," said Zenze.

Staffnurse frowned angrily, corked his hands into the pockets of his greatcoat and sat staring into the empty space under the table.

A tall, thin African policeman came into the shebeen and lowered his gangling corporal's uniform down on the bench next to Liquorice Boy. He paid for his brandy—being off-duty—and poured out a large, neat tot from the half-jack he'd been given.

He looked hard at Staffnurse for a minute, wondered where he'd seen that coat before, leaned over to him with a surly sneer and said: "Don't do it again, bokkie, don't do it to us. Perjury, nothing else."

He joined in the political talk half-way through his bottle; gave it as his own idea—also off duty—that "the man must be bleddy mad"—meaning Mnr. Kob.

"Just look how hard it's going to make my job, boks," he appealed to the men in the shebeen. "O.K., so now we don't only have illicit liquor charges; but this'll mean arrests for illicit marriage and illicit education also. The kids'll go along to special shebeen schools to learn reading and writing. Brother, they'll have to bleddy double the bleddy police force."

Staffnurse allowed his friendly face to be pulled into a large scowl. His greatcoat stood up ferociously around his ears. Then he dared to pop his head out from behind its protection for a moment to say to the company in general: "If every guy doesn't become a police, the Government can't keep he's laws, hey?"

A question the policeman felt it necessary to answer on behalf of the Government. Turned to Staffnurse; drained a heeltap of brandy through his skimpy moustache; pushed the bottle and glass over to Staffnurse; and said: "Bokkie, we got to keep those other damn kind of laws, haven't we? If we wasn't here who would stop any man from murdering your wife, who would see that the fellows had their passes, who would. . . ."

"Yah, Mister Constable Corporal Shabalala who would of stop us buying yeast for the beer last year," asked Sadie tartly.

Zenze, the political theorist, explained carefully to the cop that, firstly, Staffnurse had no wife, secondly that it was a crime against the people to force them to carry passes, thirdly in preventing real crime the police were almost useless anyway, because they were too busy "propping apartheid".

"Jus' not so busy they don't find time to walk in for a drink in every shebeen, if they's not raiding it and closing it down," said Sadie, her professional interest adding to her ordinary political tartness here, to put an edge on her manner sharp enough to flavour her strongest brew.

Another matter the policeman felt obliged to answer. He tapped the greatcoat on the shoulder to summon Staffnurse's head out into the open again. "Bok," he said to him, "you can bleddy sue me if I ever close down this shebeen. It's run good, the liquor is clean, the customers is respectable, not to mention the Ma, and, of course, in fact, it's hardly illegal."

Staffnurse grouchily retired back behind his defences, not having enough quick words to use against the policeman.

Zenze left the policeman to his hardly illegal half-jack and got back to the Bill. He gave a fine analysis of its ugliest features, then examined the motives behind its author, Mnr. Kob, and began laying down a cautious strategy for attacking the Bill, its author and its supporters.

The final stages of the plan involved tough anti-government action, and this, the policeman, who had been listening from the other side of his half-jack, was forced to regard as "hardly legal". He felt, this time, obliged to dissociate himself from the plotting, told the company at large: "Ge'mmen, don't do it," and walked away into his beat.

Followed soon after by that friend and close admirer of the force, Mr. Staffnurse Phofolo. This Mr. Phofolo aired himself in the great odorous cloud of the sewerage farm, as a refreshing contrast, to drive away the contamination he felt from being cooped up with the police. Then he crossed over into the aura of the crayfish cannery and made for home (for Mrs. Hampshire's home, that is). Got in just before the curfew.

Here he was immediately informed by the lady herself of the great event of the day. "Terrible, Staff, terrible! If you only knew what's happen in this bad Bill!" she told him. Staffnurse was not going to spoil her story either, and put on as nice an appearance of ignorance as he could manage.

"Government say no more meetings, he say political party finish have mixed membership"—this particularly exasperated Mrs. Hampshire, who had personally press-ganged most of the dozen or so Coloured members into her party. She went on with her kitchen-English interpretation of the Bill, exploring for Staffnurse more of its inner meanings. "Oh, my boy, it's finish for African people."

"Auw," Staffnurse clucked consolingly at her, "very sorry, missus."

Mrs. Professor Hampshire felt that his sympathy greatly sustained her in this difficult time.

11

CAPTAIN BOYCOTT

A jazz song in Sesotho about the Bill had caught on in the black townships of the country. The English speaking chairman of a toilet-paper firm had turned down, as too sensational, a suggestion to name a new brand after Mnr. Kob. Afrikaans parents in the pro-Government backveld had begun a campaign to give their babies names beginning with the initials NOB, in honour of the great new Native Omnibus Bill that was to save white civilization, or K O B, in honour of its creator.

In three weeks the Bill, Kob's Nob, had become, as they say, part of the language.

Its appearance in debate, though, had been postponed two or three times, "to confuse the Opposition". This had worked pretty well, although it would have certainly been just as difficult to think up a move that would prevent the opposition being confused. Two Opposition members quickly claimed the Bill as their policy anyway.

"The crayfish-walk!" shrieked the Government members happily, "they're sliding backwards already."

That unofficial unenfranchised Opposition sitting in its shadow parliament over in shantyville had acted more sharply. Shadow might be called, but substance seemed.

Tonight it had met, and tonight it had taken action. Taken sharp action.

Staffnurse had sat in Sadie's place four hours waiting for the meeting to end. "Ag, why must they keep the poor boy sitting here all the time," said the lovely Sadie. Staffnurse would have liked to indicate that he considered it no duty, but indeed a great pleasure to wait in the shebeen.

But he couldn't get it out quite so well. "No, man, 'sokay," he managed to tell her.

And why did he find his stay a pleasure, for he sat with the same can of beer in front of him all the time, cracking away at his pennyworth of crayfish feelers and sucking the marrow out of them? It was not Sadie's beer that held him pinned there so loyally inside his greatcoat. It was not the snugness of the shebeen. It was not the company. Not the talk. It was Sadie herself. And he hadn't the words to tell her. It was not just the right pronouns he lacked now, but oh! the nouns and adverbs and delicious adjectives, too.

"It's on, Prisoner," Zenze came in out of the shadows, into the warm shebeen. There was excitement in his voice. "We're going for them this time, mascot."

Staffnurse said nothing, waiting to find out exactly what was "on", who was being "gone for".

"Yerp," Zenze slapped his fist in his hand, "queues in shops first. All shops that don't play fair."

"All?" asked Staffnurse.

"Yerp." Second slap. "And newspapers."

"And?"

"Yerp." Slap. "If they don't use the word African. And jams."

"And?"

"Yerp." Slap. "If they don't use non-white labour. And cigarettes." Slap. "And cigars."

"*And*? Wow."

"Yerp." Slap. "Same reason. *And* cakes, *and* cold drinks, *and* tea, *and* razor blades, *and* other things." Slap, slap, slap, slap.

"Wow!" Staffnurse said feebly.

"It's a general boycott, from food to drink, from Cape Lusikisiki to Mount Sukunikuni, from now until victory."

"Wow!"

"We decided like this," Zenze began to explain while the wowser expired weakly inside its greatcoat. "They bring in their new Bill, there's absolutely no way we can protest or do anything political any more. All the people are angry, so now's the time to act. Throw in everything, instead of a slow building up. Give everyone a chance to join the boycott. Simple."

"Goin' to join!"

"Fine, fine. What you going to boycott?"

"Goin' to boycott—everything."

"Everything?"

"Zactly."

"I'll be working here, not Port Elizabeth," Zenze added off-handedly.

"Why?" Staffnurse looked shocked.

"Ah, well, I suppose I'm not good enough for the big job there."

"Good enough before."

"Yah, well," said Zenze easily.

Staffnurse won't let him off like this. "WHY!"

A quiet minute. Then Zenze leaned his head towards Staffnurse, said in a whisper: "Son, they don't trust me."

Staffnurse was so shocked and angry that his small command of words expired entirely. Instead he glowered. From behind his black face still blacker looks glowered out at the world.

"They don't feel sure enough it wasn't me who got in touch with the cops at the Parade meeting. You can't blame them, I was the only one away early."

Staffnurse clearly felt able to blame them. Blame them for short-sightedness, lack of faith, disloyalty, general inefficiency and incompetence in the presence of the enemy, and worse.

"Dube", he pushed the name fiercely out from among the blacker of his looks.

"Oh no, oh no," said Zenze. "Dube! You mean he's been saying it about me."

Staffnurse said nothing more. He looked so black now he just as good as disappeared into the shadows. He screwed up his eyes and nodded knowingly, very knowingly, at this word "Dube", but he said nothing. Absolutely nothing at all.

"Yah, well, anyway—I can do some pretty good work down here. And you can help me," said Zenze.

The black look kept nodding away knowingly and ominously, though it allowed a dim smear of light to shine from it for a moment at the thought of helping. Nodded away and screwed up its eyes.

"My girl," called Zenze to Sadie, "a straight of brandy."

He drank his brandy. Staffnurse had another pull at his can of beer, now in the fifth hour of its life (and not improving with advancing age). There was no one else left in the shebeen; Sadie was at the far end of the room, knitting. They sat quietly for fifteen minutes, puffs of smoke coming from Zenze, short little curt little nods coming out of the shadows from Staffnurse.

Staffnurse stopped abruptly in mid-nod. "Everything," he said in an attack of talkativeness, "everything," and slapped his hand in his fist.

"Everything?" asked Zenze once more.

"Everything—excep' books," said Staffnurse.

A bar-lounge in Parliament still shaking and echoing to the first impact of the Bill. Members plotting over it, Members feeling it out for flaws, Members examining it from this side, then walking over and examining it from that. A very senior Member deciding he will not speak on the Bill for fear of committing himself. A very junior

Member committing himself to making a name by planning a tremendous speech on the Bill; a very alcoholic Member making up his mind to commit himself, there and then, to the principle of a second gin before the debate. And a very long-necked Member cycling up and down the lounge looking for a table that will admit him to its round of drinks. It's that well-known parliamentary cyclist, Parpenfus.

12

POISON DUST

Horse-tails of dust curling up from the tops of the mine-dumps; blowing up to the city; spreading across the pavements; coating the washing on the lines of the poor; and even—with an impudence that knows no social distinctions—settling on the half-acre desks of the mine-owners. Dust so fine and blown so hard it penetrates everywhere; makes its way into the works of watches; shows up inside the most tightly-locked of strongrooms; and even—with an ignorance that recognizes no scientific facts—insinuates itself into the insides of the pies and sausages, as if baked there by the cooks. Fingers feel it, teeth crunch on it, nostrils trap it.

This is the dust from the soil that does not nourish, from the mine-dumps of the great Witwatersrand. It contains the gold that does not nourish, that settles in great armoured vaults. Like the stone Stock Exchange, which it also falls upon, the golden dust does nothing to pay its way; it feeds no one, clothes no one, houses no one—but clogs up the veins of the city and spreads its film over all. Only in the Stock Exchange is it lovingly regarded, for there it has fed a few (too richly), clothed them (too smartly) and housed them (too ostentatiously by far). And on the desks of the brokers and the mine-owners it seems to spread just a trifle more richly, knowing that there it will be protected.

On the desk of one of the mine-owners it lay in a three-day thickness, for this man, Mr. Bargoyle, M.P., had been all of those three days down in the Cape "in the public interest".

This phrase, which sounded well, meant that he had transferred his money-making powers from the "private sector" to the "public sector". There was only so much he could do in controlling his gold and diamond and industrial interests at company level. After that there had to be control at government level. It was still of course in the "Bargoyle interest" but carried on in the public sphere. He had to be in Parliament personally to plead for lower taxes; bigger quotas, fatter licences, more labour.

It was Friday now, and Bargoyle was due back to start his week-end a trifle early. Already three African building boys had been summarily dismissed for omitting to clean the dust off his desk and were on their way back to the kraal; already three secretaries had been driven off their heads devilling speeches he might want to deliver that week-end, preparing accounts to indicate how much his companies have been earning for him in the week he was away and getting up to date his political file to tell him what had been going on down in Parliament while he was there, lest he had missed anything when he was on the telephone to Johannesburg, finding out what was going on up *there*. And a fourth secretary had been sorting out the notes on chess in the daily paper and analysing them for him for quick study.

For he was a tiger for work, and no idler who sat by while his millions did their own growing. The millions had to be prodded and activated, fertilized and hoed, and generally forced along and matured. The chess had to be pursued just as effectively and efficiently. He slogged at it hard (and so did his chess secretary), he slogged at his tennis and his private conversations and his bazaar-openings.

He might have taken his week-ends early, but he certainly took them seriously. A fine fellow and a worthy millionaire, thought the Stock Exchange with hardly a dash of envy.

At eleven a.m. sharp, Bargoyle, followed by his coal-black valet, stepped off the Cape plane into his waiting car. He was handed the latest 'change quotations in one hand and the next morning's chess problems from the *Daily Times* (which he owned) in the other. He liked to keep one jump ahead of the market, and one move ahead of the readers.

He looked in his pocket for a small stick of nougat there, nibbled off the end and settled down to his jumps and his moves. The driver said nothing, the valet said nothing. Bargoyle said nothing, but slogged away. He was in a fine condition and had the market licked in ten minutes and Black mated in eight.

At eleven-twenty he stepped out of the car and stepped on to the pavement, to make for his half-acre desk inside his one-and-a-half acre building. Nearly stepped on to a legless African, looking up at him from ground level. The man seemed to be lurking there, waiting for something—which agitated the white doorman enormously. "Go away, go away, *voetsak*," the doorman screamed.

The African went away—rolled away, slid away, skidded away—dragging himself along on the tiny platform on castors that served him for legs. The platform, made of wood, was strapped to his torso, where his legs should have begun. On his hands were two old shoes, which paddled him along the ground. The whole object was slightly less than three feet tall.

He tobogganed along a few yards, pivoted agilely around with a squeal of castors, leaned his broad back against a bus pole and watched Bargoyle disappear inside, followed by his black servant. The doorman disappeared inside, too. Then the cripple disappeared inside after them, dragging himself up the steps and into the great building.

But only for a minute. A hysterical shout came from the doorman, who struggled out again with the legless man in his arms, the two cracked shoes clasped around his neck. He dropped him on the pavement and almost collapsed, sickened at such closeness to such horror.

All this time the cripple said nothing, showed no feelings. Now he frowned in a puzzled way, waited a minute still in doubt, then rolled and scraped away; around the corner, along the street, until he came to his beat on Rissik Street, where he reclined on his platform and put himself to his trade of horrifying the population into supporting him. A few small coins rolled towards him during the day. He thrust them into a pocket of sacking that hung round his chest and continued to frown.

His "customers" were all white, the blacks were hardened to horror, except for one man—it was the black valet—who came past with a dour-looking black woman and stuffed a note of writing paper into the sacking. When no one was near, the cripple took the paper out of his sacking, looked at it hard, smoothed it out and put it back. The frown was gone.

At six o'clock, when the last shoppers had gone home, a small bedraggled handcart was trundled up by a small bedraggled boy. The cripple, with the boy assisting, got into the cart and was wheeled away to his home.

The home looked much like the owner. Many of its essential parts were missing altogether, others were deformed and the whole thing was generously hung about with sacking. But the home, at least, was not abnormal, for most of its neighbours were in just such a state of patch-and-sacking too. Inside the house of Lebane, the cripple, was waiting a well-dressed, immense African, a man whose beard had turned into a curly fringe which was trying to creep its way around the lower half of his face. It was Induna.

He held out his hand to Lebane. "Come on, old post

office," he demanded. Lebane paddled up to him. Out came the notepaper.

Lebane smoothed it out once more, then stretched upwards and handed it over. "Fourpence to pay," he smiled "airmail, no stamps." He added in a whisper which Induna had to bend right down to hear: "I first thought it was the white man."

Induna took the note, gave him another in return, told him to keep it until an Indian woman came for it in the street. Then he added a friendly thud on the back that sent Lebane rolling along on his platform with small squeaks, and left by the little home-made shanty door. Lebane's wife lifted him up on to a paraffin box, anchored him there, then gave him his evening porridge. They talked humbly about the great man who had been with them.

Induna was on his way to Cross Street to the African Congress of Equality offices. "Quality!"—they gave him the thumbs-up sign as he walked along. Africans darted out of shop doors with their thumbs raised, delivery cyclists wobbled in the middle of the road as they lifted their thumbs from the handlebars, a Coloured driver leaned six feet out of his passing van, yelling "Quality" at him, and further rows of thumbs, looking like ditto-marks to all this, appeared at the windows of a crammed-full green bus to the townships.

"Equality" he murmured back at them and walked into a chemist shop on the corner. He nodded, smiled his quiet, warm smile at the little white man behind the counter, went behind a partition, and felt his way down some dark, palsied stairs.

The meeting was waiting for him downstairs. The meeting of the A.C.E.'s Transvaal leaders. Induna had come up a few days previously to transfer his strength to the biggest centre of population.

"We did not intend to go so far so quickly, brothers," he told them, "the boycott was to have had a slow, steady build-up, we would train as we went—but this new Bill that Kob has introduced forces a change of plan on us. The Bill is a declaration of immediate war and we've got to take it up as seriously and earnestly as possible. The full-strength boycott is our only way of retaliation; there is not even any chance of our making a protest to them in words any longer; they won't listen.

"The Central Executive decided a few days ago when I was still in the Cape to take this stand. We didn't yet fix a date, though. Now I have a message from them: the date of the calling on the people to boycott is the date the Bill passes its second reading—that is the date when the rulers will show themselves determined to put it through.

"So we have a few days left to organize. . . ."

The meeting went on with its discussions, while it heard the nervous white "sympathiser" whose premises it was using, scampering about in his shop above.

13

BADGE OF QUALITY

Equality badges were spreading out over the face of the land like an umbrella of locusts—red locusts. In every town and village the red badges were being cut out and sewn on. Simple badges. Just red silhouettes of Black Africa. Ready for the boycott.

On Sunday at Orlando in Johannesburg, 25,000 of these badges had marched their owners along to Home-town Square and were getting a word of advice from Induna (through the mouthpiece of an unbanned speaker) about the boycott. In Durban the meeting had been banned before starting and the badges had gone off to the soccer instead. Thousands more of the badges were standing close together in the rain at Korsten, Port Elizabeth, paying close attention to the sombre speech of Dube. And in Cape Town they were jumping and jiving to the fighting, inciting ideas of The Flea of Africa (who might have been in Dube's place at Korsten.)

The flea was tickling them, irritating them and nipping

them into action. Into action the next day, when the second reading of the Native Omnibus Bill was due to end and which was to be the first day of the Great Boycott, all over the country.

There was a particularly distinguished badge sewn on to the pocket of a distinguished greatcoat which was watching the special secret police at the back of the meeting taking down notes of the instructions given to the crowd, and watching the Press at the front of the meeting taking down notes of the plans for the future. "The quicker the spread," Staffnurse thought to himself almost maliciously.

He edged right up to the police as Zenze came towards the end of his speech, stood aggressively near them and gave an aggressively loud handclap right in their ears.

His performance was admired by the surrounding Coloured youngsters who giggled and pushed and nudged themselves and Staffnurse until they all sprawled on to and over the seated detectives. The detectives hit about them at everyone within range, cursed about them at everyone out of range and looked in a particular way—hardly *friendly*—at Zenze and the other speakers who had caused them to be called out to work overtime on a Sunday afternoon.

After the meeting, the tall Zenze and the short greatcoat with its crop of peppercorns advertised on the top made their way to Sadie's, bobbing along beside one another.

"Do you know!" said the greatcoat on an up-bob.

"Uh?" said the Flea, drawing level on the next down-bob.

"This detectives . . ." said the greatcoat, touching its badge absent-mindedly.

"Uh?"

"You know what. . . ."

"Uh?"

"She's going to be very busy after now, I think."

"Yerp."

"She's going to be very, very cross."

"Yerp!"

Sadie's. Sunday night. A drink of Carry-me-home-to-die for Zenze made that day by Sadie the Lady herself, distilled from fermented pineapple juice (and, so it was said, carbide). A large glass of warm water for Staffnurse, to keep the cold out.

"Got to go now, chief," said Staffnurse, draining the warm water in a brave final swallow, "take professor out."

"You be leaving him some-a-wheres, mascot?" asked Zenze, very casually.

"I reckon."

"Couple hours?"

"Reckon."

"Oh, fine, fine, boy, then you and me kin take a little ride some little place."

Staffnurse looked away, studied the other corner of the room and hummed tunelessly.

"Well, Sadie, I guess we got somewhere we got to be getting to go to," said Zenze, standing up breezily, and downing his bottle of drink.

Staffnurse stood up too, staring gloomily and uncomfortably at nothing.

"So I'll come along with youse, young Prisoner," said Zenze heartily, as if it had all been settled.

"Can't say," said Staffnurse, as if it hadn't.

"Oh, come now, my boy, you can't just wait there two, three hour."

"Then I gotto take car back."

"Sure, then I kin come back with you, eh? No law against lifts?"

"Yah, can't go ride some little place."

"Oh, no, no, just ride back with you. Just maybe ride around a little. Jus' little."

Proposition not carried unanimously—one junior member voting against.

"Look here, boy," said Zenze, turning serious, while he poured himself a farewell tot, "this is business. This Congress business now, jus' got to ride around little see a coupla guys about coupla critical matters. Jus' ride around coupla little guys."

Staffnurse was miserably caught. Zenze graciously paid his bus fare in to fetch the car, hung around in the hedges until the professor had been carried to his dinner, and climbed aboard the Chev on its return.

"I think we first have little drink," said Zenze, "what say Sadie's?"

Back to Sadie's to fill their tanks again with Carry-me-home-to-die and warm water.

Zenze disappeared from the shebeen for a moment, came back, topped up with a double tot, yanked

Staffnurse up and the two of them boarded the Chev again.

"Town," said Zenze tersely, "and a yo ho ho."

Staffnurse started off.

"Whoa ky," said Zenze, "one tiny drink first." He rushed in and out. "Yo ho ho ho," he said.

They got on to the main road—an arm waved from the pavement. "Taxi!"

Staffnurse was driving on. "Give the poor guy a lift. No law against lifts, eh?" said Zenze.

"I wonder, I wonder," thought Staffnurse to himself, humming soundlessly while the man climbed into the back, "I wonder if they's laws for lifts."

> *I wondering, I wonder,*
> *I wonder what I wondering . . .*
> *Boo-booooooom.*

He scratched his head slowly: "Chief," he said to Zenze, "I wondering. . . . I wonder. . . ."

"Wonder what, kid?" asked Zenze.

"No, I forget," said Staffnurse.

"Oh," he thought to himself, "I wonder if they's any laws at all, I wonder."

"HEY BOY KEEP ON WATCHING WHERE YOU GOING," said Zenze sharply, and he came back with a crack, and steered across to the left-hand side of the road.

They got to town, Zenze called out "three bob" and the man handed over some silver to him.

"That goes into my Congress pocket," said Zenze looking hard at Staffnurse and funnelling the money into his whipcords with his left hand.

Staffnurse looked back hard at him.

"Okay, boy, back to Windermere," said Zenze, "The quicker the turnover, the quicker the profits, the fatter the funds, the sooner the freedom, better the people, happier the Africa."

He suddenly started singing: "Happy, happy, happy Africa," under the influence of his bootleg liquor. He turned serious: "You got nothing against Congress, eh, boy?"

Staffnurse didn't think so.

"A-bingo-bingo-bingo-bing," concluded Zenze.

Staffnurse turned back to Windermere, they picked up another two men, Zenze took another silver collection, he took another little drink and he was then ready to spend another substantial period at Sadie's.

"You want another quick drink, you young Prisoner?" Zenze asked Staffnurse.

Staffnurse thought about the warm water for a bit and turned down the offer. He walked out towards the car and started to drive off.

"Hey, bo, jus' a mo," said Zenze running out, "you not going to drive away with *this*, are you?" He steered himself cautiously round to the front of the Chev and pulled off an enamel sign reading "Second-Class Taxi". "Much better you keep it hid in your boot." He tossed it into the car, grinning amiably and blearily and clambered back to the driver's window.

Staffnurse stared back at him sadly. "You put it!" he accused.

"Sure, collect funds for the boycott, my son," said

Zenze. He shook his left-hand trouser pocket; it jingled wealthily. He shook the other pocket: silence. "Well, so long, I'm trying for another small one," and he disappeared inside Sadie's.

Staffnurse threw the taxi sign into the car's boot and drove off to fetch the professor.

14

BRIDE PRICES

"We are not talking about that, my friend, we are not talking about that. Not about that, not about that a-tall," said Proprietor W. Twitch, "not a-tall, a-tall a-tall." Mr. Twitch seemed to be completely clear on that point. "A-tall".

The man he was talking to, an uncle on the other side of the argument, a Mr. Bonzo Shabalala, uncle of Corporal Shabalala, was completely unclear. To him that was what they *were* talking about, if they were ever talking about anything a-tall.

It was a set-to between opposing groups of uncles and aunts over the bride-price for Mr. Twitch's fifteen-year-old niece, Fancy, prominent and long-legged veteran of a recent Battle of Waterloo. For the long-legged, sweet-faced Fancy was to be married to the longer-legged long arm of the law, Corporal Katz Shabalala. And conversely Corporal Katz Shabalala was to be married to Fancy—if there was agreement over the bride-price and the terms of payment. It was a matter for the family to strike a bargain.

With this in view, the party of the bride's side, Mr. W. Twitch, Mr. W. Twitch's wife, his brothers and sisters, his wife's brothers and sisters, the brothers' and sisters' wives and husbands and where available the wives husbands' brothers and sisters—every possible shade of aunt and uncle—were there. Only Fancy herself was missing. It would not be traditional for her to be present at conferences on her *lobola*, her bride-price, in any case it would be inappropriate in one so young, my dear, her uncle from the Transkei had mentioned to her. (Nobody mentioned to anyone that it might be inappropriate for one so young to find herself married).

Ranged against them was the avuncular might of Shabalala's family. Not to mention his father and mother, or his father's brothers and sisters, or his mother's brothers and sisters, the brothers' and sisters' wives and husbands and where available the wives' and husbands' brothers and sisters.

The proceedings were taking place in the main back-room of Mr. Twitch's shop in Windermere Location, where, as the notices on the wall said on the one side, "Out of Hand Sales conducted Daily Prop. W. Twitch", and on the other, "Out of Hand Sales conducted Daily Use Springbok Salts."

The more important uncles and aunts were sitting in the shop backroom but the overflow of the less important and the cousins were accommodated in the shop itself, where it was sitting among the stock of one and a half bags of mealie-meal, a half bag of sugar, a broken show-case containing five loaves of bread, seventeen bars of Lifebuoy soap, fourteen packets of President cigarettes, four packets of another brand discontinued these eighteen months and two cheroots which on the proof of their condition should also have been discontinued immediately; and various small quantities of children's sweets, jelly powders and cold drinks. Not a large stock, certainly not as large a stock of goods as there were present a stock of cousins, but then Mr. Twitch had a small bank account that matched the stock very fairly.

The proceedings had begun early because there was only the one day to be devoted to this business of bride-price and there were a lot of aunts, uncles, cousins and others to get through.

It was just before seven o'clock in the morning, in fact —yet before we had cleared our throats properly, before we had begun to make the proper tribal courtesies, before we had begun to enjoy ourselves at all, there was a knock at the shop door and a small customer came in. It was a very small customer, about something just under four feet, but a customer nevertheless, and customers did not figure in very great numbers in the books of W. Twitch. He—the customer—was passed over the heads of the crowd, so to speak, until he reached the counter, where he was served, with some deference, by "a close relation of the proprietor himself", one of the uncles on the bride's side.

For a small customer he had a very big order: half a loaf of bread, half a pound of mealie-meal, half a dozen eggs and half a bottle of paraffin. He paid for it all in a collection of coins of the minutest denomination and was passed out over the heads of the crowd again followed by his half portions.

The crowd of aunts and uncles settled down again, made further preliminary rustles and waited for the prospective bride's senior uncle and guardian to name a figure for the *lobola.*

The crowd waited—because another knock came, and another customer entered; and another close relation of the proprietor attended to him. The proprietor himself and his immediate family were puzzled at the large amount of business for the time of day—and rather hurt to tell the truth. A shop was a good enough proposition of its type, thought Twitch, but no one wanted it to occupy too much of one's attention. Make it your slave, not your master, was his philosophy.

There was a third demand for bread and sugar, an unsatisfied demand for the morning newspaper, for fruit and fresh milk, and then the business of the meeting was allowed to proceed.

"We were not talking about that a-tall," Twitch reminded Mr. Shabalala, "the fact that the young man is a police makes no difference to the relatives he marries into. A police gets good pay, but, well, he's a police."

There was no denying that, it was clear that a police was a police, and Twitch got on to indicating the points of the valuable young woman they were offering, referred to her straight back and legs, reminded the opposing uncles and aunts that there were not many young women of such well-known virtues in the average Location these days and added the information that educationally she was very advanced; had passed two subjects of the upper primary level and would've passed history too but for difficulty with dates.

There was immediately a counter-attack by the Shabalala faction, launched by several old tory uncles who felt that this was over-education, that any girl who knew as much about life as that would make no one a good wife. She would always be hankering for more money, would not obey her husband, would no doubt refuse to take a beating regularly and would be most likely unable to keep a babe on the breast through unnatural, civilized, sanitary and hygienic squeamishness.

"My old mother used to work right up until the minute she had her babies and right on from the minute she'd had 'em," said an opinionated uncle who had worked forty years in the municipal service under the name of Johnny Water-and-Light-Account. "As a matter of fact, at the time she was carrying me she was so strong and healthy that no one knew she was going to be delivered, until, while she was pushing the bread into the earth oven with the long baking pole, I suddenly arrived. On the ground. Didn't get my first feed until the bread was done."

"I remember the days," said the oldest Uncle, "when there would be huge beerdrinks after the birth of an infant. A-times, on the other side of the Fish River we had enough calabashes full of beer to drown a dozen elephants."

"Ay, and the elephants were there, too, in the old days," said old Silas November, "my father told me of the elephant hunts he used to go on. I could tell you: the elephant's tooth I have here" . . . he patted his pocket where his magic anti-rheumatic cure was kept . . . "I got from father."

Some half-hour later the conversation, interrupted by eight more calls from customers, had extricated itself from the Fish River and the old days, and the bride's side, which acknowledged the drawbacks of education, added in mitigation that Fancy's school reports all concluded with the phrase Could Do Better.

By now it was the middle of the morning and the main argument had come near settling—the price should be Sixty-Five Pounds, in cash, cheques or cattle.

The groom's side, still making elaborately long faces to indicate that they were being asked to pay too much for the commodity, made a movement, even more elaborately, to rise from the conference table and leave for home.

"But, wait, wait, wait," shouted the Oldest Uncle.

"Hey, hey, hey," shouted the cousins.

"My dear sir," said in effect Mr. Twitch, as senior uncle and leader of the bride's case, "isn't there something you forget?"

"Forget?" said an elaborately puzzled groom's faction, eyebrows rather shooting up above the level of their foreheads, "Forget? Surely not a-tall," and continued to get up with many stretches, groans and yawns.

The bride's side shrieked louder still. Leading counsel

thundered out that the whole bargain had to be considered cancelled, that this was no way to do business, that when *he* was a lad, etc., etc. Yes, and when *he* was a lad, said old Water-and-Light-Account, etc., etc.

What, in fact, asked Mr. Twitch, were the arrangements the groom's men were going to make for a special small present for the father. Wasn't it traditional? Was tradition going to be discarded?

"Oh, the father!" said the other side deprecatingly, but Silas November and other senior members of the groom's side were stirred by this call to tradition, and it was agreed that the groom's side should settle down again, which they did with further groans, stretches and yawns, back among the diminishing stock.

"Shall we say Five Pounds?" asked the groom's side.

"Five Pounds!"—the shriek was on.

Hardly had things got into a comfortable way again, when they heard "ko-ko-ko" from outside. The shop door opened and three women came in together to make purchases.

This was enough. Twitch bellowed at them: "What's the matter, buy, buy, buy all day long." Hadn't they anything better to do, their houses to look after, their children to care for, had they gone mad for trade?

The women giggled, but stayed to buy. Bread, tinned milk, mealie-meal, they ordered, and a bottle of fruit juice.

The order for the sophisticated article fruit juice, which had never been in his stock, infuriated Twitch. "Fruit juice, tfooh!" he said, spitting on the ground. "White man's piss! Go to the white man's stores for that.

What's the matter with the white man's stores anyway. There's mealie-meal and bread there also. Why do you all come and buy here!"

The women giggled. Then they looked serious. "Old man, don't you know what's today? Don't you know why we buy from your sick old shop? The boycott has started."

For a minute silence.

Then, "Quality", shouted a dozen or so of the younger cousins, from the back of the room, "Africa!"

For a minute uproar.

By lunchtime the conference had shaken itself back from politics into duty again. The argument turned onwards to a shawl for the mother (also absolutely laid down in the traditions according to the beliefs of the bride's side). By now the stock of the shop was sold out completely, except for the cold drinks and one of the cheroots, after the temporary political boom. The uncles and aunts were able to settle down to the remaining details uninterruptedly. Six of the youngest cousins were posted outside to warn off any further prospective customers. Four of them rushed off to join the boycott (if a boycott can be joined) but the other stayed behind on the picket-line.

The conference weightedly got back to business. Well, now, what about a sewing machine for the bride herself. And kerchiefs for her sisters?

And what about swagger sticks made of the best polished tambutie wood for the four brothers of the bride? . . .

This was a boycott that everyone was joining (if a boycott *can* be joined). Its very first foundation and inaugural member in Cape Town was a mass of patches knitted into the shape of a coat, which answered (from deep within it) to the name of Staffnurse.

Staffnurse rushed off from work, without permission, to Windermere Location, to help superintend the non-buying of goods. He okayed this shop or that, directed large crowds round to Twitch's place as a philanthropic and friendly gesture and exhorted the public in its ones and twos not to let down the A.C.E.'s boycott. He mentioned himself as a fine example of non-buying, of new greatcoats, for instance.

Staffnurse headed a great procession of Location urchins who were also pointedly not buying greatcoats (or diamond rings) this day and all dashed off to the edge of the town to see the fun. Among the troupe were the eight famous survivors of the Battle of Waterloo, excused from family *lobola* debates by their age.

They came to a grocery shop on the corner of Eighth Street and Gross Avenue. A famous shop for ignoring fair play in queueing, a famous shop for pushing "Jim Fish" into the back rather than keep white customers waiting. Suddenly the shopkeeper found he didn't have to keep his white customers waiting at all. There was no embarrassing crowd in his shop, no shoving, no chattering, no discomfort any more—and practically no business.

Just one African customer was left standing at the

counter, the little old woman with the teaspoon dangling from her neck; she hadn't yet cottoned on to the idea of boycott.

"They haven't any gratitude at all," said the shop-keeper bitterly, speaking over his counter and the head of the little African woman to the white woman he was serving, "allow them in your shop and they'll be wanting to sit down in your own living-room next and drink your beer." He was ready to go on and mention that "they" would be expecting to marry your daughter after that, but the white woman left and he was not ready to swop his opinions with the old woman or her teaspoon.

The old woman bought her threepenny packet of salts, walked out and was met by the deputation of black kids and Staffnurse. She immediately got into a furious attack of spitting when she realized just how she had been scabbing. She told Staffnurse the conversation that had been coming from the shopkeeper, almost hurled her packet of salts back into the shop at him, thought how it might react on her health, spat in his direction instead and wandered off to the Location, muttering to herself that in *her* opinion, if anyone wanted to consult *her*, it was clearly a white man's world.

Staffnurse walked into the empty shop himself, while the children clapped their hands over their mouths at this startling and treacherous behaviour.

He humbly went up to the shopkeeper and said: "Want bottle beer."

"Uh?" said the shopkeeper, "washu wan' ginger beer?"

"No, baas," said Staffnurse, "beer, want beer."

"Beer?" asked the shopkeeper, irritably.

"Yes, baas; beer, living-room."

The shopkeeper grabbed at him, just pulled a patch off the greatcoat, but Staffnurse escaped otherwise intact and tumbled back among the urchins who all scattered, tripping over one another and screaming heartily at the fun.

They ran off down the road, leaving one six-year-old crying far in the rear, quite convinced he was due to be overtaken and arrested for contravention of the Shops and Marketing Act.

15

HAPPY, HAPPY AFRICA

The gang trotted into the main part of town in a broad front, sweeping up four or five coloured kids and one Indian too, as it went. Made for Adderley Street to see the big shops and what was going on there. Got stuck at the Grand Parade for eight minutes while it watched a cheapjack selling a set of genuine gold candelabra—only nine-and-sixpence each—decided firmly against buying one; volunteered *en masse* to guard a car that was pulling up, didn't get picked for the job, made a new application for the next car, didn't get that job either, and decided to go out of the car-protecting business right away. In fact felt it was a racket rather than a business. Considered the bag-carrying business; rejected it too on account of the total absence of bags. Suddenly reminded itself that it was on a political mission and marched on again to Adderley Street. This patchwork army, led by its distinguished greatcoat general, had by now attracted another three pairs of torn trousers, and one made-over flour bag (finest grade flour), and had also pulled in by its gravitational influence three smartly-tailored white youngsters who had been parked for a minute on the square by their parents. The whites, being a well-drilled bunch, soon found themselves promoted to near the head of the ragged rabble. They were graciously allowed to change their grey worsted shorts for three of the more outstanding outfits, including a pair of someone's Father's employer's near-deceased slacks re-jigged to hang from the shoulders by string, and were taught the right way to shout the boycott slogans.

The big stores were all very quiet, Staffnurse saw with the one eye that wasn't needed for controlling his army's passage across the robot. By this first afternoon almost all the non-white population, Africans, Coloureds, Malays, Indians, had caught on to what was wanted of them. They had spontaneously gone further; it wasn't just the shops with complete colour bar that they walked past, but even those with minor discrimination. And how a non-white can sniff out the slightest scent of discrimination.

So now they were having a harder time than usual, even, queueing in long lines outside the few stores—mostly Malay-owned—that passed the test.

The whole Staffnurse troupe joined one of these queues, just on principle, moved slowly up to the counter, smiled politely and walked away, finding that it didn't have so much to spend anyway. Chased by the shopkeeper, it dashed up past Government Avenue, where several of the squirrels seemed to be in mind to join the demonstration. Slats of wood had been picked up, tissue paper collected and the army soon formed itself into a percussion and paper-comb band. When not engaged in active boycotting it performed before white shoppers, mulcting them of a few useful pennies that might have gone into tills.

By the end of the day eight-and-sixpence had been raised. It was carefully invested in a round of ice-cream sodas bought off the uncle of one of the Coloured kids and they all strolled back to their shacks and slums. The white recruits having been very generously permitted to keep their string-and-slacks and having timidly offered their own worsteds in return, were disbanded and sent back to the Parade with instructions not to buy anything on any account ever again until all the laws were changed.

Staffnurse led his remnant of Waterloo veterans back to Windermere, where they found the family party at last broken up and nothing left in the shop or house to eat that evening, except possibly a boiling of cheroots.

Over to Sadie's Staffnurse went, to wait for the Human Flea. Sadie, who was in a great state of excitement over the boycott, gave him a friendly kiss on the part of his ear that was protruding from the collar of his coat. This so overcame him that he sat down right where he was, which happened to be next to his great hero and model of perfection, Corporal Shabalala, squatting on the bench with his hand round the neck of a pint of brandy.

"Trouble," said the corporal gloomily, peering behind the greatcoat screen, "trouble it'll bring us, this nonsense of the not buying." Having himself splurged fifteen pounds as the down payment for a bride that day he felt entitled to being righteous about mean spenders.

"Trouble?" said Staffnurse, looking at him cheerfully, feeling the poor man to be more misguided than malicious, "not buying is not trouble." Staffnurse put this precept into practice on the spot by not buying a shot of brandy, and thus not getting into trouble with Sadie for not paying for it with money that he did not have.

"Hundred per cent Durban, Port Elizabeth, Johannesburg, Kimberley, all stations to Cape Town." In sprang the Flea, just back from an emergency joint executive between the A.C.E. and the hurriedly-formed Boycott of the People. "The Joint has been promised support from the other Congresses; two rich Indians have offered a truckload of potatoes to boycotters; Yerp and there's a big white-owned store already got up a banner 'Any race colour or creed' and already it's been positively queued to bits. And the shares of Consolidated Bazaars who haven't got no banner, they've dropped at the Stock Exchange."

Staffnurse, who had almost emerged from his greatcoat in excitement, slapped Corporal Shabalala on the back in the middle of drinking his pint, shook the Flea's hand warmly, turned back to dry down the Constable's coat and beamed and winked at Zenze over his shoulder.

"And the suburbs bus boycott here has started already. Hundred per cent," said Zenze.

"But," he added, starting on a brandy-and-beer,

"whites in Evaton have strung together to boycott the Indian shops, they even stoned one of them, and the friendly white department stores in Port Elizabeth. Also Pretoria."

Shabalala waved a spiteful constabulary finger at Staffnurse: "Trouble," he said.

The trouble didn't seem to offend Staffnurse very greatly. His smile continued to shine out all over his face and over most of his greatcoat as well.

"Trouble," roared Liquorice Boy Kekana hoarsely, pounding his right fist into his left hand, "trouble is what we'll give 'em." He triumphantly took a swig from his tin of powerful skokiaan, brewed that morning by Sadie herself, let it slide down his throat until most of the larynx must have been burned away, and even more hoarsely, roared out again: "Trouble!"

"Yah, you'll run to Rhodesia," sneered Shabalala.

"We'll *all* be in Rhodesia," said L.B.K., with a mighty generous sweep of his arms, "Yeah, boy, yeah, boy," and he broke into a snatch of a Louis Armstrong song, now that he'd got his throat properly sandpapered.

"Yeah boy," he rasped and jumped into a heavy jive in the middle of the floor. The rest of the shebeen's patronage immediately jumped in after him, while Staffnurse sat back clapping two flat bits of wood together to keep the time, and thinking thoughts of warm ginger beer. Sadie rushed around from one shiny piece of furniture to another to steady them down, but when the crowd started on the busy rhythm of "Skokiaan" she could not keep out any longer.

"Oh, happy, happy, happy, happy Africa," she sang, high up in her soprano register, while the men, stamping their feet this way and that together, chorused a low, ominous doom-doom, doom-doom.

"Skoki-skoki-skoki-skokiaan," Sadie sang the song of the shebeen queen, telling how the people would warn one another of police raids for illegal skokiaan stills. "Doom-doom, doom-doom, doom-doom," went the men.

Sadie danced too, kicking her strong round legs and her skirts right over the shiny furniture, her breasts leaping about inside her blouse as friendly as you please. "Doom-doom, doom-doom; doom-doom, doom-doom," sang all, "a-bingo, bingo, bingo, *bing*."

This was followed by a special L.B.K. version of the old marching song: "We are dancing to Rhodesia," that lasted quite thirty-five minutes, and then Zenze stopped the jive to teach the whole company the words of the new Boycott Anthem.

Down they all flopped to get on with the drinking except Liquorice Boy who had turned his jive into a musical shadow-boxing exhibition. Then he too collapsed.

Shabalala finally walked out, staggering rather grandly inside his uniform, after his bottle (less the spilled portions) had been drained.

Zenze could get down to confidential gossip about the boycott with Staffnurse. Told him of the terrific hold-back of buying in Cape Town, mentioned a couple of shopkeepers who had been out into the street looking for customers, persuading them that they would all be treated "like gentlemen", and mentioned a report that had come in to the Joint office of a sturdy little troupe of youngsters that had been wandering through the city keeping up the boycotters' spirits and had even formed itself spontaneously into a band to collect money for the movement.

"Even," echoed Staffnurse weakly.

"Some white kids with 'em," said Zenze proudly.

"Some," echoed Staffnurse feebly.

"It's the little things that show the people are behind us," said Zenze.

Zenze had another little illicit beer stiffened with another little illicit brandy, arranged for Staffnurse to meet him at the Joint the next evening for boycott work, rehearsed the company present once more in the Boycott Anthem and sprang off into the wet night again.

Staffnurse waited for another peck on the ear from Sadie and trotted home to the Hampshire outhouse. There he sneaked the Chev out of the garage and spent two hours driving the bus-boycott travellers home from the station. Stuck up in front was Zenze's sign SECOND-CLASS TAXI.
The money went into his left-hand trouser pocket.

He was roused by the shrieks of Mrs. Hampshire in the morning, went in prepared to apologise for his recent absence, but was immediately set to packing up Mrs. Hampshire's belongings ready for the early afternoon train back to the Rand. And his own belongings, too, if any.

"Staff," said Mrs. Hampshire earnestly, "You people

suffering; oh, suffering too mush. They start big boycott, I go back Johannesburg fix boycott."

"It could have a salutary impact, Staffnurse," Professor Hampshire added importantly.

Staffnurse started the household packing, did his own packing between two gulps of tea, scratched his head hard about getting a message to Zenze, was still scratching it when the train pulled out at two-thirty p.m., and settled down in his third-class coach next to the engine to wondering exactly what Mrs. Hampshire was intending to do about the boycott and wondering whether a salutary impact was a good thing or not. This called out his last reserves of head-scratching and left him with a wider furrow than usual between the quadrants.

16

BITTER TRIANGLE

The first free minute he got, back on the Rand, Staffnurse loped off to the Joint's national campaign headquarters, pulled a peppercorn in salute to Induna, gave the thumbs-up sign all round, and reported for orders.

Orders? First to stick pins in a map showing where the main local offices were. Second to count the funds collected at a weekend meeting. Third to look after the baby of the wife of a member of the executive. Staffnurse felt vaguely that he'd held this job before somewhere. Fourth, to escort Induna on a tour of the central area. Which they did in disguise, each with a basket of naartjies for sale and the banned Induna dressed up in a shabby grey suit and a greasy cloth cap. Staffnurse felt somehow that his own disguise was almost perfect, it might merely be necessary to pull the cotton reel out of his ear to make him less conspicuous.

What a wild, vigorous boycott he found here. Not the

rather jolly, gentle affair of Cape Town. Johannesburg, with its crazy, glittering, gilt-edged character, was doing this in style, too. In the parts where black and white townships joined there were clashes between black and white gangs—the police were out, the papers were screaming news of the boycott, the English papers screaming in particular about the shock to the share market and the Afrikaans papers screaming in particular about the shock to the nation and demanding that the Government step in.

"Son," came from the huge, shabby grey suit as it walked on next to the small greatcoat, "we've got to act decently all the time. We can't let up. If a white mob gets out of control it's just juvenile hooliganism, but if one of ours does, it's rape and revolution. Got to see we don't have any hooliganism. Got to see they don't force us into hooliganism."

"Going to see," said Staffnurse.

They walked along, watching the inconspicuous pickets, the irritable shopkeepers and the armed police.

"She shilling-shilling," said Staffnurse to a white woman who was insisting on buying some of the naartjies.

"Oh, madness," cried the woman. "This boycott has sent the prices crazy." She flounced off distractedly.

There was never such a wide smile at the loss of a sale as shone out from the darkness of the greatcoat. Then it turned back to Induna, switched itself off at the mains, looked grave and understanding and continued its walk.

They circled back to H.Q. and Staff was excused duty.

He took a bus up to Sophiatown and sat inside Chops's room, waiting for him to get back from work. In the next room a new record was on, but it had already gone through a very efficient ageing process and was sticking at a good few favourite spots.

What a reception he got when Chops came in: first of all of course a great, happy, giggling laugh and a hug; then a fire put on in his honour; then convoys of small boys summoned in from the shacks in the yard and sent off to bring water, to buy pies, to lay in brandy and one very specially deputed to buy ginger beer; then the inter-leading doors thrown open for the music.

"Ko-ko-ko," came from the doorway. Ttsotsi gangsters strolled in to nod a hello to him. There was Two Boy Sevenpence whittling away sadly, Alfred the Great, Alexander the Great and the others.

"Been up de river again?" asked Boy Sevenpence, "what'd day frame you fer dis trick?"

"No," said Staffnurse, "been Cape Town."

"Oh, so, and you see de inside of Roeland Street jail? Sure say it's got nuttin' on Number Four. Number Four's got de higher walls, smaller cells and tougher warders. Hey, we lost Alf the Great there for a little while; but dey couldn't keep 'im. Why should dey, he's a good boy; dose cops never get no witnesses say anything 'gainst Alfred, hey, dey friends of mine, dose witnesses; sure and dey wanna stay friends. You notch on, hey? You let me know next time you in Roeland Street."

"Yah," said Staffnurse, finding it easier that way.

The small boys were returning with their cargoes and seating themselves on the floor next to the door for any possible leavings. Just the one boy was missing—the ginger beer boy—but he came back, too, with hands full of ha'penny fat-cakes.

"Say," said Chops, furious, "I told you ginger beer, not fat-cakes."

"Yeah?" said this young learner-tsotsi. "Boycott."

"What?" said Chops, more furious, "cold drinks is boycotted, not ginger beer."

"Ginger beer is cold drinks," said the boy, "so I get fat-cakes instead. What you want ginger beer for, you got brandy, ain't you?"

Chops spluttered wildly, then lifted his head up and laughed and laughed. He threw the cakes at the kids and turned to Staffnurse to talk boycott with him.

"I goes and buys a tin of jam the day before the boycott," said Chops, "then I goes and don't open it yet, 'cause I'm out at a party; so early on Boycott Day I take it back to the shop and change it back. Yah, I got this Boycott working both ways. But listen man," he said to Staffnurse, "these kids are pretty fine too. Not one of them," he waved a finger gravely, "not one of them bought any piece of soap *all week.*"

Boy Sevenpence and Alfred the Great had a political problem, Chops told Staffnurse. What exactly was the ethical position about commodities they—ur—confiscated in the way of their business? To boycott or not if they came across goods that were on the list? It seemed a pity, they felt, when certain stuff was left absolutely lying about, so to speak.

Staffnurse thought, Staffnurse scratched a patch of his hair quite threadbare, Staffnurse retired right inside the greatcoat to meditate—and Staffnurse found some brilliant counsel there. He translated counsel's opinion for the tsotsis: anything found "absolutely lying about" that figured on the boycott list could be taken but should not by any means be kept for private use or conversion. It should be sold and the proceeds—all the proceeds, cautioned counsel, who seemed a suspicious fellow—should be handed over to the Joint Fund, anonymously.

This solution brought an outbreak of cheering from all sides, Chops laughed until he coughed, coughed until he cried and then started laughing again through his tears; the gang members looked admiring; the kids at the door ran round and round the room in excitement, arms spread to their full wing-span, shooting up police vans and dive-bombing stocks of boycotted goods. Two in their further excitement treacherously became police motor-cycle escorts and the battle continued in the yards where the bikes rode up and down, exhausts burping and sirens blaring. Finally aircraft, vans and motor-bikes all had serious back-fire trouble and retired to a shack in the yard to scrape bits of dried porridge-skin from a pot left there.

Staffnurse bussed back to H.Q. with Chops, where they worked hard helping Induna until late in the evening. Queries from Joint offices were coming in from all parts of the Reef and reports from all parts of the country.

There was also an urgent request, turned down after some thought, from Congress men in British Bechuanaland to join in the boycott.

Lebane, the cripple, had been wheeled in to see the chief and offered to move his beat right into the main entrance of Rissik Retailers, who had been particularly nasty, and act as a picket. He said with a grin that he felt he might have a more powerful effect at frightening off customers than the usual boycott demonstrators.

Five minutes later five white women (ladies, the messenger believed) were announced in an impressed whisper.

Staffnurse withdrew into the depths of his coat and managed to scuttle out of the way before he was spotted. For, prominent among the five—to the extent of being positively outstanding—was his own Mrs. Hampshire.

These liberal ladies came to the point immediately. "Who's in charge here," they asked severely, rather as if they were expecting to see a "responsible" white man.

They were given Induna's deputy to talk to; straight away offered to run the boycott for the Joint, "but of course it would have to be on a much more limited scale" . . . offered their help as advisers when the first proposal was turned down politely, and offered their cars, chauffeur driven, when that was turned down.

Then they sailed out again, having "fixed" the boycott as far as they had found possible and sailed home in their chauffeur-driven cars. With one of the ladies, in the boot of her car, sailed home also a Boer War Greatcoat, once officially pensioned off but still quite ready for a last campaign or two.

Staffnurse was Mrs. Hampshire's sacrifice. "You go take car, see Boycott people, work for them two days, work very hard, you help your people that way."

Staffnurse tried to look reluctant.

"Go quick-quick."

"Quick-quick," agreed Staffnurse, glad to get the green light.

He polished the Chev briskly, sought out his taxi sign and drove off to the townships.

Before the day was done he had been on five up-trips to Orlando and five down-trips and had netted £4 5s.

This was handed in at the office; "Is from my Mrs. Professor," he said.

He went off to Sophiatown for one more trip, parked his car near the terminus of the boycotted bus-line and waited for passengers. One of the buses stood there waiting too, but with much less hope. On the pavement near him sat three aged, rounded African women, buttock to buttock, legs in the gutter. One he recognized as Two Boy Sevenpence's tough old mother.

A pale-faced Coloured man in a great hurry was coming up to the bus ticket office, and passed between the iron queue-bars.

"Those who ride today," said the one old woman, turning to her neighbour, and suddenly raising her voice, "I will be sorry for them."

The coloured man slowed down, looked around uncomfortably, grinned weakly, and hardly able to make up his mind, went up to the ticket-window.

"I'm worried for them," said Madame Sevenpence, peering down hard at the darning she was doing, "I'm truly-reely worried for them when they wives find out what's happened to them. I think it's their throats where they get it."

The pale coloured man didn't look in quite such a hurry; but he had his ticket in his hand and made for the bus.

"Throat," mouthed the other old woman greedily, "you think that's all; such a crowd of people catch them in the night when they come back, they's nothing left from them; throat, eyes, ears, fingers, hearts, liver, everything; when they come back at nights," she ended with a big sigh, hardly able to think about all of it.

The coloured man looked alarmed at last. He glanced down at his watch, turned towards the bus, went paler than he'd started as for a moment, and came running over to Staffnurse.

"How much to town?"

Staffnurse scratched his head, while trying to work out what was double the normal fare for one passenger. "Seven shilling," he said brightly.

"No, just single journey," said the coloured man.

"Seven shilling and six," smiled Staffnurse evilly.

The coloured man looked back at the three mothers of the nation, gulped and climbed in.

The greatcoat found itself confined to barracks for the

next three days and its news of the boycott confined to what it could pick up from the newspapers. It led a little private boycotting of its own, in its capacity as Assistant Household Buyer for the Hampshire Organization.

It travelled miles to a sympathetic white grocer when sent out to buy a pint of milk, it insisted on this rather than that brand of tinned foods and it was quite unable to find any cigarettes in stock anywhere at any time.

What Staffnurse picked up slowly from the newspapers was that the boycott was growing bigger and stronger all over the country. Even way out in the reserves whole tribes were enrolling and forcing their political and social demands on storekeepers and local officials.

The newspapers were themselves taking no chances of being boycotted and changed their style, referring to Africans instead of Natives, putting Mr. before their names and generally being more respectful than before.

Here and there enlightened whites accepted the points of the protest and were themselves accepted again as sellers to the public "by appointment".

But national problems of supply and demand were getting difficult to equate. Already some associations of wholesalers had decided to withhold their goods from African retail shopkeepers, in retaliation, and were talking of doing the same to the whites who had "come round".

Groups of Africans were finding themselves hungrier than usual, and this was making them angrier than usual. Groups of whites in the commercial and industrial trade were finding themselves making less profits than usual and this was making *them* angrier than usual. The police, trying to keep the peace between these two angry groups, only had as much success as to make themselves angry, too. So there were three sets of lost tempers chasing one another around the country.

17

IT'S WAR, MESSIEURS

Great sequels to the boycott! Parliamentary parties had blown up, reformed, settled down again; Parpenfus had wheeled himself alongside the aged Prime Minister and told him with a knowing wink: "Prime, I know a good man if you're ever in need"; Pumpernickel had given up history and begun a study of company law, Hampshire had decided to undergo another lunch. Of course Kob was up to something. Spurred on by the shopkeeping world he had an amendment to add to his famous H-Bill, before it was yet through Parliament.

"I just want to add one clause at this stage," he said, peering at his papers in a good show of absent-mindedness, as if this were something small in an administrative way and not the business that had kept the Cabinet up after midnight all week, "Yes, here it is, it's a clause affecting situations such as might arise from the present commercial anti-buying campaign and could well prove useful to the police.

"It's been drawn up of course purely in the interests of the natives themselves."

Out came the clause—to ban all boycotts, to punish and ban all who boycotted, organized boycotts, incited boycotts, demonstrated in favour of boycotts and even gave power to punish and banish those who were merely "not buying anything" if they were "deemed" to be "passively boycotting".

Mnr. Kob, looking quite charmed with the idea, sat down while half-reading through another paper on his desk, in a far-away mood. The public in the gallery said hoarsely to one another: "Just one clause."

The M.P.s in their benches said to one another "Just one clause" and walked outside arguing loudly. Again the parties blew up, reformed and settled down in new line-ups. Parpenfus back-pedalled quickly over to his original side, Hampshire cancelled his lunch and Pumpernickel fell into a long shallow sleep during the debate.

Just one clause, they all confided to one another, as if that made it all the more horrifying.

Great sequel to the clause. Just that one clause was enough to kill the boycott dead where it stood.

"So," said a Qualityman at the secret meeting of the Congress executive, "We've got to stop the boycott. End it. Then, boy, we move fast some-a-wheres else. It's war, messieurs," he said drawing himself up dramatically with a hand pinning up an invisible cloak around his shoulders. "To the ramparts!"

There was a tendency among the members to rush out

and look for the ramparts, but Induna gently giggled at them. "Surely, yes surely we must move fast somewhere, if boycott is prohibited with such a fierce prohibition," he said, "but I think that once again History is writing itself for us, and we don't have to do anything foolish. We are not taking these decisions at all, old friends. We can only act as principle tells us, rightly and honestly and honourably. It is the Government that takes the decisions; it is History that is hurrying the Government on towards its earlier destruction and disappearance." There was a round of rather more sober applause for this.

"Now I find," said Induna with his twinkle pressing its way into prominence once more, "I find that History had laid these following plans down for us.

"We cannot boycott any longer without committing suicide. So we withdraw our boycott forces, without any casualties, with a good few gains up and down the countryside and with no loss of prestige. Yet if after that we sit back and do nothing we may begin to lose prestige, we lose face.

"All right, sires, we are not tiresome and traditional and can ourselves stand a loss of such an inessential article as the face; but our great movement has to keep the respect of our people and they might lose heart as well as face—a far more serious loss, I think you'll grant."

They did grant, freely.

"What we must do is to move onwards to the next stage of the great plan," said Induna. "A general stoppage of work. A two-day stoppage is what I can see in the history books our grandchildren will read. There is something more written there too—but that I can't quite see yet."

The meeting was completely satisfied and hugely cheered by this great plan. They felt that History was a sensible fellow, with a bold touch. They decided to wait for three more weeks before announcing the plan, until Parliament was "up" for its six months' recess, so that no more "little clauses" could be added to spike them, and to set the stoppage down to start on the Monday.

"Yes, Monday," said Induna with a chuckle, "the people will like a long weekend."

Still two weeks to go before the House was due to be up, and Staffnurse got orders to go to the airport to fetch the professor.

He and the Chev stood and sparkled in the sun while the professor took his seat in the back. "Welcome, baas Professor," said Staffnurse.

"Oh, welcome, my boy," the professor returned, thoughtfully muddled, "welcome, indeed."

The Chev pulled away carefully, anxious not to jog the professor.

"Look here, Jackson," he said rather furtively, "do you know why I'm back early?"

Staffnurse looked around, making his face show polite interest, while his mind set into order a few stray internal thoughts: "I wonder," it said to itself, "if we got petrol. I wonder," it added, "if we got any air."

"WATCH WHERE YOU'RE GOING, YOU INCREDIBLE PRIMITIVE OX!" bellowed the professor.

Staffnurse's head whipped round to the front again, he steered adroitly between the airport's ornamented gateposts.

The professor breathed hard for a minute, chewed over his anger, swallowed his swearwords at birth and re-digested the anger juices that had been secreted in his system. Gradually he began to produce warm friendly juices again and a smile began to twist itself into life underneath the shelf of his nose.

Staffnurse meanwhile switched back to his thoughts, but couldn't pick up the thread. "I wonder," he frowned fiercely at the white line down the middle of the road, one eye shut in concentration, knowing there was something he shouldn't forget. "I wonder if. . . .

"Boom-boo-boom-boo."

"Do you know," asked the professor in a kindly tone at last, "do you know why I'm back so soon?"

The head, wondering profoundly what it had been wondering about, started to turn around politely, froze suddenly and instead shook itself positively beneath its chauffeur's dashing naval cap, to admit ignorance.

"Disgraced, my boy, back early in disgrace; suspended from the House for two weeks."

The cap tried to shine a sympathetic look towards the professor through the back of its head. The Chev drove more carefully than ever.

"You call it disgrace?" said the professor, beginning to laugh a bit.

The chauffeur's cap nearly shook off the head trying to deny that it had ever used the word.

"Hu, hu, hu, hu," laughed the professor, holding his small round stomach between his arms as it wobbled up and down around his diaphragm, "hu, hu . . . yet is it disgraceful to be suspended for calling a Member faithful? hu, hu, hu, hu, hu, u, u, u, u, u, u, . . ." he went on, sobbing almost, until the Chev began to consider a course of shock action, to bring him out of his fit.

"I want you to consider the empty Lobby of the House, my dear Jackson," said the professor, when he'd recovered, "a harsh howl coming from inside the chamber to mark the 'performance' of Kob's Nob—you'll take my meaning—when suddenly the door opens and an Honourable Member is ejected backwards, still talking angrily. The serjeant-at-arms follows in a precautionary way.

"Now, Jackson," he leaned over to the front seat and added softly: "Consider that this Honourable Member is me—I, I should say; no, me—and consider that I am grumbling to myself that I see nothing unparliamentary in calling a Member faithful. Do you consider all that?"

The head and cap shook themselves smartly to indicate that this point had been carefully considered.

"Well, Jackson, there you have the stage set. Let us go back into the chamber with this ejected Honourable Member, to see what caused his ejection—ejectment?

"My dear fellow, we are debating this H-Bill when Van Muckle, that rare iniquity of a wool farmer, interjects that the Bill will serve to keep the kaffir-lovers in place as well as the kaffirs. (Jackson I use his words, not because I approve of them, but to give you the tone of the argument.) He looks over with his head stretched at me and shouts: 'And you know where that place is, Mr. Speaker.'

"I reply perfectly courteously, perfectly softly, perfectly unprovoked, 'There's a place for him too, Mr. Speaker.' He screams at me and bleats out: 'Mau Mau'. I get up on a point of order and ask, purely in the interests of order, whether the Honourable Member is not supposed to be here to represent the views of his constituents, rather than of his sheep—and whether in fact he ought not now to be returned to the faithful flock from which he had sprung.

"I felt this to be a very parliamentary way, Jackson, of putting comment, a very carefully selected word 'sprung', but it draws a great row from their junior whips; our whips get up to row them back and Mr. Speaker halloos right out above them: 'Who called the Honourable Member a sheep?'

"The Government backbenchers howl and whistle, the Government whips leap up in a single unlovely body. I rise, myself. The howling continues. Then it at last begins to quieten down. 'Who,' repeats Mr. Speaker eventually, glaring at me, 'called the Honourable Member a sheep?'

"There is complete silence," Hampshire continued, " 'Who called the Honourable Member a sheep?' he demands again.

" 'Mr. Speaker,' I say, 'is the question not being asked here in quite the inverted order, quite back to front, as it were?'

"Do you know the word pandemonium, my young friend? Well, I think you could well remember it from today. Pandemonium *descended* on the House, if I quote the Press correctly."

He sat back blissfully in his seat, a tiny smile winking over his face. "Pandemonium having died down," he went on, "I would still, naturally, not withdraw the ridiculously flattering way of referring to Van Muckle—so I am out of the House for the final fortnight," he finished off rather smugly. "Extraordinarily flattering," he grinned.

They drove on, passing through the Location area. Suddenly an African in plus fours, walking under a big golfing umbrella carried by a youngster, held out his hand at the Chev and shouted, "Taxi, taxi, taxi, taxi."

Staffnurse straightened up in fright and the Chev shot ahead at a great speed—they'd both remembered very clearly what it was Staffnurse was wondering about.

"NOT SO FAST, NOT SO FAST, NOT SO FAST," screamed the professor.

The Chev hurled itself around the next two bends, then stopped in a skid.

Staffnurse darted out to the front of the car and began to tug at something there.

"What's it now, what's the trouble?" called the professor irritably.

"No, baas professor, just sheck petrol," said Staffnurse, his head smiling above the front mudguards, very ready to please.

"Petrol, you ground ape," said the professor, not highly

enough trained as a mechanic to question the position of the petrol tank, "leave it till we get back to the residence."

"Yah, baas professor, sure."

He meddled with what he was pulling for another minute, the professor began to work up his adrenalin content, shut his eyes for thirty seconds, opened them to see Staffnurse still attacking the front of the car and clambered out to watch him.

"Yah, baas professor, doan come here, got him now," smiled the face.

But the professor came on.

Staffnurse yanked the taxi notice off the bumper just as the professor got around to the front, hid it behind his back, and ran round to the back.

"What in the grotesque heavens are you doing now?"

"Just sheck oil, baas professor," said Staffnurse from the back, opening the car boot, and throwing the notice in.

They came to the Hampshires' house, the Chev drove eagerly up the jacaranda avenue and made for its garage and the professor hurried to the front door, just as Mrs. Hampshire came out, panting: "Maxie, Maxie, what have they done to you?"

"There, there, old girl," he patted her as she clung half-crying, to his arm, "we haven't at all disgraced ourselves."

"Jackson," she sobbed over her shoulder, "you go way, go way!"

Staffnurse discreetly left for the back of the house.

"Oh, Maxie," she wailed.

"Oh, now, now, now, Lida, for the sake of peace let's not get sentimental and pious," he said testily, "let's call it an honour."

His sharpness made her gloomier, her gloom made him sharper, until they began to shout at one another. This immediately caused her a minor asthma attack, which he ignored while walking into the house, studiedly reading the evening paper.

"In any case," said Mrs. Hampshire between her breaths, from her basket chair, which showed little fat balloons of dress pressing through the holes, "it's time you were more of a pleasure round the house when you do get back instead of sitting there scowling to yourself."

Hampshire pulled his lumpy nose out of the newspaper with such speed it made a faint pop. "How can you see what I'm doing here? And in any case, a fat lot of good you are to a man," he shouted back with as much relevance as she had managed.

Mrs. Hampshire made a retort he could not catch, though he sensed it was uncomplimentary. He was just about to fling back something at her quite as uncomplimentary and certainly quite unparliamentary when instead he subsided in his chair and said in a grey voice, counting his juices to himself and looking down at the floor over his peptic nose, that she wouldn't be so sharp with him if she knew how he'd been disgraced. "Parliamentary career ruined. . . ."

Mrs. Hampshire looked over at him anxiously and waddled straight over to comfort him, straightening out the little gridwork of balloons that had impressed themselves on that part of her where she waddled most. Hampshire muzzled into her with a sob.

"I didn't mean to be gloomy," she said.

"I didn't mean to be grisly," he replied with a sniff.

Then she kissed him tenderly on the nose and remarked that it was always the thing about him that she loved the most. He patted her on her behind and made a similar confession.

Hampshire pressed the bell for Staffnurse and asked him to bring the brandy. He poured them each a brandy, added a quarter-bottle of lime to his wife's so that she could not taste the brandy in it, and added another three fingers of brandy to his so that he could.

"I sorry to tell you go way," said Mrs. Hampshire to Staffnurse. "Baas professor work very hard for your people in that place Parliament, he's getting too mush sad."

"All right, Jackson," said the professor, "I must add that I regret to say that the Bill passed all its stages, even such efforts as mine did not avail, and is now law. I regret to say it, my boy."

Well, here come the rest of those Ministers and M.P.s, clerks and hangers-on again; back to their files and their urgent business and their avocado-pear plants, all rather satisfied with themselves for having broken the back of the boycott; but back they come also to more trouble than they have seen before.

Mnr. Kob himself found out the news in a special personal "informative" memo given him on his arrival at the Pretoria station by a member of a large bunch of senior officials. But he bought the afternoon paper and there it was anyway—blazing across the front page: "A.C.E. calls General Strike. 'Holy fast, not defiance' claim organizers."

That made Kob frown. That made Kob angry. That made the officials wish they'd not bothered to come to the station to impress him. Because it looked as if the plan had been deliberately formed to keep out of the grasp of the new law, ready-made for fitting on to any serious opposition to government. Even that newest, slickest H-Bill was too low-powered to trap and convict anyone found praying.

Staffnurse found out the news in an official memo from the Duchess of Hampshire, delivered by her own person. She stood him to attention in the kitchen with the rest of the servants. "You will all," she addressed the fine body of men importantly, "be interested to hear that as a protest against the unhappy condition of your people, there will be a two-day general strike. You will all remain away from work on the first day, Monday, as a mark of support. Naturally as you are not paid by the day, but by the month, your salary won't suffer."

She held her head up bravely: "As for the Master and myself—we will manage on our own somehow. But for all of us in this house, the strike will not of course continue on the Tuesday."

Nobody said anything. The brigade was dismissed. Staffnurse rushed down to the Congress office to report once again for duty.

18

HOLY STRIKE

A holy fast it started as. The first day of the strike ten million people stayed at home, doing that religiously at any rate. They prayed or not, as they felt things, and addressed words to the 217 Gods of the 217 sects they belonged to. Some called at their relatives' houses and addressed cans of home-brewed beer. But they kept away from crowds; they didn't attend meetings, didn't provoke trouble, didn't incite the whites.

Staffnurse arrived at the A.C.E. office so early on Monday morning he might almost have been had up for breaking the previous night's curfew. It was not the usual office, but a new spot picked out to trick the police should they have been thinking of coming along to raid the strike centre.

A quiet, secret little group was already working away at organization and sending instructions to the other provinces as well as to other offices on the Rand.

Staffnurse and Chops were given a packet of stickers:

"Strikers don't give in to the police—but don't get into fights with them". They rushed off into the cold early morning with the stickers. Under his greatcoat Staffnurse kept his packet. As he got to each corner a frozen black arm would come out of the depths of the greatcoat; it would carry a piece of paper up to a wide mouth, where a frozen pink tongue would lick it. Then it would be slapped and stuck on to the nearest wall, window or lamp-post.

Across the road Chops was doing the same.

They went all the way along Market Street, from Diagonal to Von Brandis, then back along Commissioner, pasting their stickers on to the centres of the largest windows of the largest department stores, just where they would strike the passers-by most—and just where they would annoy the shopkeepers most.

Out of the corner of its eye, the greatcoat spotted a large black policeman marching behind Chops over the road.

Staffnurse darted into a dark shop entrance to hide himself and the greatcoat and sang out: "Brother, there's trouble."

Chops looked across, couldn't see anyone, started to laugh; looked around, could; stopped laughing—and ran for it.

The policeman ran for it too.

Staffnurse ran for it too. He ran around the next corner, stopped suddenly, and ran back again, head down, right into the galloping policeman.

The policeman was big and bulky, far bigger and

bulkier than Staffnurse. But the policeman hadn't planned what was going to happen. Staffnurse had. He picked himself up quickly, while the cop lay on his back holding his damaged stomach and trying out a combination of a grunt and a whistle on the early morning air.

Staffnurse wondered, on his way back to the office, if he himself had been obeying the stickers' instructions quite precisely. "Still, wasn't zactly a fight," he thought.

By this time the newspapers were out. Half out, that is; struggling and panting to get themselves out. The editorial staff had helped the printing staff and the clerical staff were helping the circulation staff. Strange young white men and rarefied young girls were standing at the main corners, where black sellers usually stood, and offering their abridged strike copies.

Staffnurse importantly went up to one of them, and offered her a threepence. The timid girl was puzzled, not quite certain if it was legal for blacks to buy newspapers; but being timid, anyhow, she handed over when he looked fierce.

A proclamation, from Mnr. Kob. It warned all strikers that every possible measure would be taken to keep the peace and to keep the wheels of industry going. In particular it warned all Government employees who took part in the strike that they would be instantly dismissed.

Staffnurse whistled at the drastic step, considered whether his own position was that of being a Government employee, decided that on the contrary he was an Opposition employee, but whistled again anyway in sympathy with the thousands that would be affected.

He took his copy of the paper back to H.Q. to allow the important people a chance to whistle at it too.

Then he and Induna changed into their naartjie-seller camouflage again and did a round of the central parts of town and of the city factories. In town there was almost a holiday air; blacks living there had streamed out to sit in the winter sun on the pavements and the whites who didn't work had gone shopping.

The shabby grey jacket and the greatcoat could hardly move for the pressure of the new leisured classes, who were very keen to buy their naartjies, even at Staffnurse's inflated price of "shilling, shilling".

The factories were quite silent or were sending out single little whines as a machine here or there was set going while a white mechanic idly turned out a doorstop or an ashtray for his home.

Then, later in the day, over they trudged to the Government's railway workshops. Here there was more activity, some battering of bent boiler-tubes, repairing of coach-bodies, painting of engines. And even numbers of scattered African and Coloured labourers scampering around among the whites, working on the battering, repairing and painting projects.

From out of a greatcoat at the fence emerged a scornful arm, to point a scornful finger at these non-white workmen. But a shabby grey sleeve patted the greatcoat on the back. "Mascot," said Induna, "we can't be too angry with these brothers. They'll really take the knock if they stop work today. There'll be no job for them on

Wednesday. They've got the real conflict, all heaped on their own heads. We can try to persuade them, but we can't blame them if they are weak."

Staffnurse withdrew his finger, but that smile of his didn't open so wide that there was any danger at all of his face falling in half right at that moment. "*Must* be strong," he said fiercely.

On their way back they bought the afternoon paper. Another Kob proclamation. This time assuring the employers that they would have every assistance from the Government in whatever drastic action they wished to take—a hint to threaten dismissals too—and assuring the strike leaders and other "trouble-makers" of the Government's especial attention in the future.

"I think they will offer us each pensions, that's what this special attention means," said Induna with a wink at Staffnurse.

They walked back to the office through the knots of jolly long week-end loungers.

Into the official Congress office, where Staffnurse was sitting on the morning of the second day of the stoppage, walked a young white man. About nineteen years old, fair crew-cut hair, tallish.

He walked in earnestly, went up to the first man he saw in the room and said, looking down at the floor: "I've come to help."

The room looked up in surprise, the Qualitymen stared, the stickers began to curl at the edges and Staffnurse's eyes shot out of their sockets.

"I want to help the African people. I feel it's my duty to throw in my lot with them."

"What's your lot, boy?" asked a senior member when he'd recovered.

"Come, come, go on, go on, go on," shouted another member sourly, waving him away.

The young man stood his ground shyly. "I've joined the strike," he said, "I think all people should have equal opportunity, and I've stayed away from university classes today in protest. Second year social anthropology," he added, to clarify the position.

The sour member waved him away again.

"Now I want to help with my spare time," said the steadfast young man. "You see, I wasn't really born here, I really came from Europe first."

"Oh, sure," said the sour man, "the European from Europe."

"Stuffness," said the other senior member, "take him away and show him what to do."

Staffnurse beckoned to the young man and they walked outside, and made for Sophiatown.

Staffnurse was staying there for the duration. He walked in to Chops's room with the young man.

They found Two Boy there. Two Boy narrowed his eyes at seeing the white face, opened them wide again at seeing his smart overcoat, took out a knife and began to whittle biltong.

"Say," he said to Staffnurse, "woss goin' arn? Wots you bringin' de Dutchman here for?"

"Not Dutchman," said Staffnurse, "striking guy."

"Strikin'? Wots he strikin' *from*?"

The young man, who'd been looking from one to the other of them eagerly to see how he was being accepted, put in quickly: "I'm striking from second-year social anthrop., actually. You see, I thought it was necessary to show my solidarity with the African people."

"African people. Ah, crap," said Two Boy, not caring for too much sentiment.

"Yah, he want do something," said Staffnurse, keeping the peace.

"Wot kin he do?" asked Two Boy Sevenpence incredulously. He turned to him, pulling out his knife again, and clicking out the blade in one movement, ending up with it practically at the young man's throat. "Kin you use a three-star, hey?"

"Uh, no," said the young man with a weak smile.

"Cleeeeeech," voiced Two Boy drawing the knife in a realistic movement across his throat. "Kin you make wid a grenade? Craaauuww-unchhhhhh-unchhhhhhh," he stuttered, spitting deadly lead, and showing a revolver nestling in his other hand. "Yack, yack, yack, poing, poiiiiiing," he went on, dropping to a knee next to the window, and taking aim at passing rustlers.

The kids from the backyard formed a junior choir immediately and began to bark at the enemy through their revolvers, improvising the noises off. "Yacketykackety-yacketykack- - - plit, plit, plit, plit, krooooooooooooo."

Two small kids were sent off on despatch bikes for reinforcements; practically toppled the young white man over where he stood, another took aim from the top of the rickety wardrobe and another curled up on the floor, dying from a particularly fatal wound in his throat.

While his gurgling death noises were still leaking out of him Two Boy straightened up and said: "Say, wot *kin* you do?"

"Well, I think I can write messages—and make speeches," he said.

"Oh, you can, uh?" said Two Boy impressed.

"Oh, certainly," said the lad, confidently now.

"Well, make a speech," said Two Boy.

The young man thought for a minute, then said in a strained big voice: "Ladies and gentlemen. . . ."

"Uh, nix," said Two Boy, "Dat's stoopid; you see any ladies here? Dey's on'y gentlymen here, boy."

"Gentlemen," said the young man, "we are gathered here today not in any spirit of self or any feeling of malice towards the world, but possibly to further those ancient virtues and moral values. . . ." He looked up to see Two Boy send a long contemptuous shower of spittle rakishly along the floor. He decided to hurry things on: "Facts, gentlemen. Government must be broken. Only way to break is to stay out one hundred per cent on this strike, white as well as black, hit back where we're hit, march forward to grand new world, where there no privilege and where there no restrictions on anyone whatever their race, colour, or creed."

"Yah, or dere sex," said Two Boy approvingly, giving a furious handclap, and setting the kids off into a burst of clapping, a howl of applause and a major outbreak of cartwheeling.

"Fine, boy, fine," said Two Boy, as the last cartwheel shot out through the doorway. "Now let's have it in Xhosa so we kin all unstan' it."

"Xhosa?" asked the young man dismayed.

"Hell, shure, you kin't be any bleddy good to us if you doan speak Xhosa."

"I s'pose not," said the young man. "I s'pose I can learn it pretty easy."

"Oh yes, pretty easy, pretty easy altogether," said Two boy.

"Oh, sure, pretty easy," said Staffnurse, "all these kids can Xhosa, and they on'y kids."

"Well," said Two Boy, "now say this when I say: 'Iqaqa liqikaqikeka e qaqaqeni, laqhau'k uqhoqhoqho laqhothaq-hothek' umnqunqo'," sounding off a collection of Xhosa clicks like waterfalls flooding, throats gargling, champagne bottles emptying and doors being knocked on "ko-ko-ko".

The young man gaped, but not a click came out.

"Come arn, now," said Two Boy roughly, "uqhoqhoqho . . . dat all means 'De skunk tumbles on its side over and over and over and down de slopes on de green grass, broke its neck, snapped its spine.' If you think it's easier you can say instead: 'Nquan' elo qaqa lingaqikaqikeki eqaqaqeni liqhau'k qhoqhoqho lighothaghothek' umnqonqo'." He ended with a loud drawing of the corks from champagne bottles. "Say!"

Not a click, not a drawn cork from the young man.

"And dat means: 'Stop de skunk from tumbling over

de grass and down de slope and breaking its neck and snapping its spine'," said Two Boy.

"I think I had better go and take classes," said the young man after a pause.

"Yeah, okay," said Two Boy, getting down to his whittling, "so long, kid."

Staffnurse took him down to the main road: "I think you can go back for work by your school," he told him gently.

The lazy mood of the strike had disappeared by now. From halfway thro' this second day it was serious. The newspapers first of all had agreed to publish an overlong, overwordy, oversober statement from the A.C.E. explaining what the black people were protesting against. Next to it, a reply, was the grim wording of yet another Kob proclamation. In just half a dozen sentences it made the whole A.C.E. illegal, banned whatever leaders had been still unbanned and imposed further restrictions on those who had previously been banned. Zenze in Cape Town, for instance, was declared "undesirable", Xele was ordered to remove himself to the country town of Alice "forthwith" and Induna was forbidden to be in the magisterial area of Johannesburg at all.

A quick tour of the town on the second day showed that only a few strikers had gone back; but messages from Durban told of a weakening there.

Worse: in the late morning news came through that a crowd of Africans in Port Elizabeth had stoned the white driver and passengers of a car that had driven along the road next to the Location. The police had been on the spot quicker than seemed possible, thirteen strikers were shot, ten of them dead; one policeman wounded.

"That's Dube," said Staffnurse bitterly when he heard the news from a Qualityman. "Allowed himself to be provoked," said Induna.

"Provoked himself," said Staffnurse. The Qualityman looked worried right enough.

Emergency meeting of the banned A.C.E. which had sunk underground another level or two. Decision taken to send out another warning to strikers to keep the peace. Action felt by one-half of meeting to be not strong enough; to "show signs of dithering". Insistence by same half of meeting that action be taken "to show we're masters." Meeting warned against precipitateness by Induna. Warning disregarded—meeting has smelt blood, in reckless mood. Decision taken to continue strike past the two days indefinitely—"until all demands are met".

Considered by Induna: "Impossible target".

Considered by a dark man: "very possible target."

Port Elizabeth incident pointed out by Induna as "having lost sympathy for cause".

Pointed out by dark man as "having gained strength".

Thought by Induna that strike could not be continued while Dube in charge at Port Elizabeth.

Thought by dark man that strike should then be continued outside Port Elizabeth.

Believed by Induna that the people were still "not wise enough, not strong enough."

Believed by dark man that people were "united enough, angry enough".

Vote forced by dark man. Won by dark man.

Acceded to by Induna.

Staffnurse walked home worried; he could see, he said to himself, that things were going wrong. Home was now Chops's room; he had outstayed his strike leave and felt that Mrs. Hampshire would have learned to manage without him for good.

Staffnurse and Chops shared the evening paper, with a group of next-door's tsotsis looking on over their shoulder. It was full of developments. The decision to continue the strike was already reported, more furious proclamations by Kob had followed and the police had been told by their chiefs to shoot at sight, if necessary. In Port Elizabeth the crowd had got out of hand again—and the police had again found it necessary.

Two Boy Sevenpence took his home-made revolver out of his pocket, twirled it around his finger and asked nonchalantly: "Say, we also gonna shoot at sight?"

Staffnurse shook his head at him; Boy Sevenpence looked disappointed, put his revolver away.

The changing political situation had brought the gang another problem, Chops explained to Staffnurse. Rather delicate, rather difficult to explain. What exactly were they to do about the strike? Should they stick to all its terms? Was it required for them to—er—lay off work, too?

Counsel for the greatcoat had no difficulty here at all

and presented its opinion with the minimum of head-scratching. Yes, they were certainly to obey the call to strike, they were definitely to stick to all the strike terms, they were categorically to lay off work.

Seemed hard, thought the wide boys of the narrow trousers.

Maybe seemed hard, but wouldn't it seem harder on the thousands of people who weren't bringing in any income at all, if the gang was to keep on making as much as ever?

Seemed fair, agreed the tsotsis reluctantly.

"Course it's fair," said Staffnurse sharply.

"Sure better tell the Shiners too and the Truth Brigade," said Boy Sevenpence, and saw to it that all the gangs got to know of the lay-off. Didn't want no one taking no jumps over them.

19

TROUBLE

Real trouble started on the third day, Wednesday. No one ever knew how it started, but no one cared much any more. The strikers had got so bitter they could think of nothing but their grievances, never remembered the good that had sometimes come to them, yes, even from Mnr. Kob's department on occasions; they were ready to stab anywhere. The police, having been attacked already, were not thinking of being gentle. If they were thinking at all, they were thinking of being as rough as possible. The white employers did not feel in any mood to intercede.

Staffnurse was trotting down Commissioner Street, his lonely earplug jogging from side to side, on his way to the Jeppe branch H.Q. of Congress with a message. He didn't know what was in the message, but he'd been told it was important. He'd tucked it away securely inside his greatcoat's inside pocket and patted it to reassure himself at least once every city block. In between the blocks he walked along, practising his special game of stepping in the middle of the concrete squares of the pavement, without letting it look as if he were trying to step in their middles, and wondering to himself, just wondering, if he'd get down to Cape Town soon to see a certain lively young lady.

"Boom, boom, boom-boom," he buzzed through his nose in time to the Wedding March—and suddenly found himself right upon a posse of one white cop and two blacks. They were stopping all the Africans on the pavement, demanding their passes and checking on every credential they could ask for. Playing to rule, finding fault with idle strikers.

From their friskings and fishings they'd already produced an illegal packet of yeast, a half-bottle of brandy, a huge shapeless bundle of washing tied up in a double sheet, which they suspected to be stolen, and parts for a German army revolver. These corpus delicti were in a pile on the corner, and queueing up in a crocodile behind it were the handcuffed owners of the illicit bundles as well as four more men and women whose work documents were found to be out of date.

Staffnurse was aghast. His message! His day-dreaming had let down the Congress! He stopped in the middle of a pace, his foot rigid above one of the lines of the concrete squares. Then he swivelled around at a right-angle like a mechanical golliwog and stepped into the door of the small shop he was passing.

It was a *boutique*, offering for sale exquisite hats to cheer up the wives of mine-owners, at prices to cheer up the manufacturers. Two exquisite young ladies came upon Staffnurse from the interior. "Hey, Jim," said the one of them, waving her delicate hands at him, "shoo."

Staffnurse, feeling police eyes on his back, instead of shooing, came forward a pace, out of view of the street.

"Shoo," said the first lady, clasping her exquisite white hands to her exquisite white breast. "What you want?" she asked him from a distance, not liking to go right up to him.

"Want. . . ." said Staffnurse, tugging at his cotton reel and looking round in a puzzled way, not quite able to identify its stock-in-trade. "Want . . . er . . ." he began to point vaguely at something that at last he felt he could recognize as an egg-basket. "Want . . . job," he burst out brilliantly at last.

"No, go away, no job," said the young lady.

Staffnurse moved another pace away from the shop entrance—in the direction of the till. The second young lady screamed, the first young lady grabbed the telephone and dialled for help.

"Can work," explained Staffnurse, the strike-breaker, smiling helpfully.

"No," said the young ladies together, their exquisite breasts heaving rapidly.

"Police coming," threatened the first of them.

Staffnurse backed to the door, saw one of the black cops eyeing him there, wondered if he'd be advised to ask the ladies to allow him to hide his message there for a while, decided not to take such advice and slowly stood scratching his head.

Suddenly he saw the black cop look away for a moment as a police riot car pulled up with a howl outside and he rushed through the door and on to the pavement before the reinforcements had got time to spill out.

The white cop saw him though just before he flashed past and put out a foot to trip him up. Staffnurse crashed to the ground, tried to spring up again but was tackled by at least half the police force.

His arm was twisted behind his back until he screamed hoarsely and he was marched towards the van.

By now, between his escort of six policemen and the door of the car there was a sullen crowd of passing Africans who'd been watching everything.

"Leave him," they shouted to the police, "go on, get back to your kraals."

The police angrily tried to press forward but the crowd stuck its ground. Meanwhile more and more of the city crowd was surrounding the group.

One section began to hammer on the side of the car and rock it up and down. "Leave him, leave him, leave him" they chanted as if they were singing a work song.

The little beleaguered police force were being roughed up. Out came their batons and they slashed about them. The crowd slyly melted away before the blows and re-formed behind them.

One of the policemen hit an old woman who was threatening him with an umbrella and shouting that he was about as fragrant as a cart-full of out-dated kraal manure and what did he mean by forcing people to work against their consciences, he and his damn Boers. His baton crumped down on her beret. She fell to the ground next to Staffnurse and he and his captors tripped right over her and sprawled in the gutter in a heap.

The crowd streamed and flowed over the three surrounding streets and pavements. It roared furiously and closed in farther. Suddenly a revolver shot went off; then another and another, sounding like thunder among the tall buildings. A mad, panicking scramble away from the police bullets started. Staffnurse, who'd got loose in the gutter, sped along the street, just about overtaking the bullets in his hurry.

The street was cleared. Remaining behind were eight unhurt policemen, two of the handcuffed Africans hit by bullets, glass from the window of the *boutique*, also hit by bullets and a small pile of corpus delicti, consisting of a washing-bundle, a packet of yeast and parts of a German army revolver. Missing were Staffnurse, eight prisoners with eight pairs of handcuffs and a half-bottle of brandy.

There was a shooting bout in Orlando also, two dead, dozens hurt; there was trouble in Western Township, the hospital burned down by reckless demonstrators, a doctor killed too; there was an angry affair at Wolhuter Workers' Hostel, one policeman, twenty-nine striking Africans killed, after they'd been refused permission to remain on as boarders.

In Port Elizabeth they were going crazy, even in Cape Town there were deaths and casualties.

Up and down Victoria Street, Sophiatown, roamed

and roared a juvenile patchwork army—but no greatcoat at the head of this one. The greatcoat, in fact, stood at the street corner, watching the army sadly. This was a wild, intoxicated army, not like the lovable, friendly group he'd controlled in Cape Town.

These youngsters, some perhaps only thirteen or fourteen years old, even a pretty girl or two among them, had tasted blood; and they'd tasted drink, too. They had crashed, in their crazy, savage mood, into the big shebeens of the township and sacked them. The fire was in them. Alcohol, jungle temper.

Into another shebeen they poured, made straight for the backyard, prodded the ground with sticks until they found the hidden tank of beer and carted it into a room in the main house.

Each child had a scaleful of the strong, sour corn beer. The leader and his girl—a strapping light-coloured youngster with her blouse and brassière right off her—sat on a chair together drinking from a bottle of brandy they'd captured there.

"I need to have a new dress, Sport," she said to him.

"Sure, sure, my honey," he said, putting his arm round her and feeling her breasts.

"Keep off," she snarled, slapping him hard across the eyes, "you got money to get me dress?"

"Got some," he said.

"And fer a hat, and fer shoes?"

He said nothing.

"Sport," she sneered at him, "why don't you go and take them for me? What you scared for?"

He looked down.

"Why you scare?" she said, drinking from the bottle. "you think you ever get into joining Torch Commando?"

"Okay," he said matter-of-factly, borrowing the bottle from her and swigging away at it, while looking steadily into her face. He pulled her to her feet. "Let's go," he said to the youngsters. He turned to look at her, and deliberately, put his hand on her light-brown breasts. She did nothing but quietly walked out after him, in front of the noisy, brawling crowd.

They roared through the town, along Main Road, up to the robot, across into the tramway, breaking windows, beating up white people's pet dogs, overturning motor-cars. They shouted the A.C.E. slogans. "Justice, Equality," they called for—but it was blood and drink they wanted.

Then the sudden arrival of police in squad cars; tumbling out, drawing as they landed, and shooting as they drew. In less than a minute the patchwork army was routed. Forty-nine African kids lay dead, Sport and his half-naked girl and their followers, twisting on the ground. Two casual spectators twisting at their sides.

Back into the cars tumbled the police and sped away.

This news thundered through Sophiatown, rocked it, shocked it. Nobody could find any fault with the crazy youngsters, not even the shebeen queens they had plundered. The fault was with the police alone. A huge sense of hatred for the police, the Government and the whole white race washed over everyone. Sophiatown became yet more violent, aimed its stones at everyone it saw, threw up barriers at all the road entrances to keep the police out, set alight huge smoky bonfires of worn car tyres at the corners and danced and clapped out a wild rhythm around the fires all night. Sophiatown was defiant, Sophiatown was at war. Oh, yes, the stoppage had really got going here.

Staffnurse slipped out of his room, ran fast down town, getting away from the frenzy.

But the shooting of the forty-nine youngsters did not strengthen the strike anywhere else. The news thundered through the rest of the country, too, racked it, shocked it. It horrified—but it also terrified. It intimidated the ten million people with its sudden unbeatable violence. The other towns and cities collapsed meekly, riots died out, strikers went back to work on the fourth day, without waiting for instructions.

Even on the Rand, in the neighbouring suburbs and Locations, the people, already frightened by the forceful measures, were quite cowed by the forty-nine deaths. They had no fight left. One by one they crept back to work.

The executive, meeting in its central city lair, found itself without a following, except in Sophiatown. It decided to move back into Sophiatown, into the heart of its strength. "We can still call off the strike and retreat," Induna tried to counsel them. "No retreat," said the dark men fiercely, "on!"

On they went, the mascot Staffnurse with them;

Lebane the legless with them, too, to act as watchman.

They passed through the barricades and settled in a slum house just a block from Chops's quarters, in Hope Street. Staffnurse left them still debating how to guide the people, and went back to his room, passing three different funeral wakes, for one or other members of the dead forty-nine kids. Sobbing mothers in black dresses, black *doeks* round their heads, sang wild songs.

Two Boy Sevenpence, chewing an imaginary roll of gum, was practising revolver shots at the wall before an admiring audience of fifteen kids. Nodded at Staffnurse, winked, said: "Shooting at sight, eh?"

Staffnurse sat down with Chops, who weakly tried out a laugh to greet him, but thought it would be simpler to open the door for music. They sat and talked about the way the strike had gone wrong.

"Too strong, they still too strong for us," said Chops.

"And our people, they still too wild," said Staffnurse, "they must learn, they must find more education."

They went to lean against the gate outside, as the dark of evening came on. There was the city to the east, sending its brassy neon winks up to the brassy moon. There were the square dark patches on the skyline where the unlit mine dumps blanked off areas of city lights. There was the green aircraft warning where the patrons of the hill-top restaurant were drinking. No one in the city now cared very much about the strikers. Work was started again. A battle in Sophiatown? Send the police.

Staffnurse listened, held up a finger. Chops listened. A shot or two far away on the edges of Sophiatown.

"Too wild," said Staffnurse, shaking his head sadly.

Suddenly there was a squeal around the corner. Staffnurse looked up—looked down again; it was Lebane, paddling along on his castor platform, at a desperate rate.

"Police," he gasped up at them from their knees, "They're surrounding the township. Soon as it began to get dark they started coming up, hundred and hundreds."

"They strong," said Staffnurse.

"But now they trying to join up their circle. They'll clean this whole Sophiatown up by morning. They going through every house and yard, arresting everyone."

"They can arrest us then," said Chops.

"But Induna," Lebane said, "man, we're okay; but he's banned. They'll put him away for years for being here."

"And they'll beat him up in the van," said Staffnurse.

"They'll hang him for sedition," said Lebane, "they'll outlaw Congress for ever. We got to keep Congress out of this mess here."

What could they do? How could they save the great man? Lebane turned impatiently in small arcs on the road, grinding the castors this way and that.

They had to make a diversion, that was the only way, and send Induna through it. He himself would make the diversion, said Lebane, what did he care.

"You couldn't do it yourself," said Chops, "needs a crowd of tough, strong fellows."

"Plenty tough fellows in the Torch Commando," said a voice from the dark, at the back of their necks. It was Boy Sevenpence. He was twirling his revolver still, Staffnurse felt quite sure of that. "What say I get 'em over?"

"Couldn't get here quick enough, nearly," said Staffnurse.

"No?" said Boy Sevenpence amused, "we'll get the Truth Brigade too, and the Fast Set, the Shiners, the Shack Bleep and U.N.O. You see if you could bring the boss here quick enough, before us. Okay?"

"Okay," said Staffnurse, "I fetch him, Lebane." But Lebane was already off around the corner, at incredible speed, his booted hands flailing away, his castors squealing appallingly.

The squeal was immediately drowned by another more appalling noise; a tremendous metallic banging from across the road, made by Boy Sevenpence. He was whacking the street telephone pole with a heavy tyre lever, using all his strength.

On and on he went until in the next street they heard another pole honking back in answer. Then much farther away another, then a fourth nearer again, and a fifth and a sixth, until the whole of Heaven was a sounding board to the metallic wail of Sophiatown.

On and on Boy Sevenpence went with his banging, though now first one and then another of the distant poles dropped out of the chorus. Meanwhile dark shapes came down the road in pairs or threes, hitching up their trousers, huddling in their coats.

"Hot Toddy from the Spoilers," called Boy Sevenpence over his shoulder to the puzzled Staffnurse and to Chops, "he won't touch a gun." He winked, "but he's a good boy with a brick."

On and on he banged though not a single answer came any longer. On and on rang out the homing signal.

"Rocky Mokoena coming in on the beam," Boy Sevenpence carried on calling out the introductions, "Bum and Clarence of the Moonlights. Used to quarrel a lot over this territory my boys and them, but, sure, we got to have a truce when it's bigger things. Ritzy, Transvaal Matches, Long Don Petersen. Baa-Baa from de Shack Bleep."

"Merry Xmas," said Baa-Baa, "and a happy New Year."

"And well over de fast," said Boy Sevenpence acidly, moving them on.

The newcomers fell in thickly around Staffnurse and Chops. Near them they could see shiny magazines being checked, knives being whetted, knobkerries and bicycle chains being swung in trial runs.

All the delinquents of the city were there. "Casey, Eke Mphahlele, Can-Can of the Wise Boys," said Two Boy Sevenpence, who had finished sending out his call sign at last. "They'se just out after two years in Number Four for dat Polly Street job. Hiram P. Chocho, leader of the E.P. Terrors, wid Fish, Mr. January and Peter, the whole of the Bus Passenger Protection Committee and even a couple of guys from the Hitler Gang and the Alexandra Hot Six. That's a jazz band, you catch on, but only part-time; they do a spot of work in de week."

"And here," said Staffnurse, returning the compliments, "is Induna."

A respectful shower of salutes came from the shadows. "Oh, Chief," they murmured.

"Now, surely, what's this," said Induna, "you aren't going to all this trouble to save me from a couple of years in a safe job with the Government, are you?"

"Boss," said Two Boy Sevenpence, "It's no trouble at all. Guess you'd do the same for us any day."

"No," said Induna, serious and worried, "I can't have you getting mixed up in politics and falling into real trouble with the police."

"Boss," said Hiram P. Chocho, coming up to Induna and holding a knife to his throat. "You keep outa dis. It's our little disagreement wid de sonofabitches police, ain' id? We don't wan no one tellin' us what to do, what not."

The troopleaders conferred for a moment or two. "Okay-doke, boss," called Boy Sevenpence, "just stick around wid us."

"Hey, you'se others," Chocho shouted at Staffnurse, Lebane and Chops, "you kin stick around too."

The whole, huge crowd shuffled off together, making for the western boundary. All around them ran a pack of kids.

The main body of gangsters walked along the narrow road, out of step, barging into one another in the dark.

"Hey, doan you crowd me with yo fat arse," said the Coloured gang leader, Mr. January, with a whispered snarl, as the man next to him joggled his gun-arm. "Ain't you got no native intelligence?"

"You shut up too quick, you half-white bastard, or I slice you in eighteen, nineteen, penty twieces," growled the spoonerizing Baa-Baa of the Shack Bleep, drawing his three-star knife with a grating click.

"Hey, hey, quit, quit, quit," called out Hiram P. Chocho, "keep that fer later when we celebrate."

Just at that moment the advance gang of kids spattered down the road and fell back on the crowd with a giggling scream. "Pollise, pollise, they started coming this way already."

The whole crowd whipped round and ran, doubled up, panting hard, back towards the east.

Boy Sevenpence and Chocho re-formed them and they tried to find a way through lower down, but here the cordon had arrived too and was methodically going from house to house, roughly rooting out and checking over the residents and breaking down the barricades. They had started little bonfires of the barricades here and there.

Staffnurse was scared and upset. They were being squeezed closer and closer into a couple of blocks. Lebane looked up at him, gave him an encouraging clasp around the knees.

Then the private army struck out for the south boundary road. The police hadn't started drawing in their cordon here, for across over the tramlines they could see an occasional pair of uniformed men, white and black, standing around. They hung around in the shadows of the shops on the north side of this southern boundary road.

General Sevenpence sent his men up and down the road in two main groups, keeping back a light mobile bunch to deploy in emergencies. He gave instructions to Induna and his civilian escort to make for a torn gap in the iron fence of Western Township over the road, when they got the word.

They waited in the dark, hardly talking. "Don't you be too scared, son," said Induna to Staffnurse. The greatcoat shook itself vigorously.

It was quiet tonight, not at all like it usually was in the Main Road, for the cars had been diverted and the trams stopped. A police officer walked slowly over to his van, got a radio report from his driver, then briskly got into action. It must have been the cordoning signal, the watchers thought nervously. "I wonder, I wonder, boo-boom, boo-boom," Staffnurse sang quietly to himself.

The officer passed messages along to the foot police, who started to cross the road, ready to close in and link up with the rest of the units.

They hadn't more than started, when firing began up the road, from the Sophiatown side, and from the other side came the yell of a shot cop. The police hurriedly backed to the shadows on their side, the officer went scrambling back and forth, while from the delinquent side where the firing had broken out came screams and threats and wild singing.

Then the whole performance was repeated lower down the road. The police now found themselves assailed at two points two hundred and fifty yards apart. They removed their two or three casualties, gathered themselves together and began to make for the assault points.

A fearful sparking and banging now arose from both sides, yells and cries came from both sides too, and just to further confuse the night, the telephone pole xylophone started up again behind the delinquents' camp. The kids were joining in.

"Right, boss, now," said Two Boy Sevenpence, and gave Induna a push as the police left a wide gap open in front of them.

Induna scooped up the legless Lebane, hung him over his shoulders like a bag of mealies and lumbered off. Staffnurse and Chops ran fleetly along at their side. The night was rowdy and no one could hear them.

They were almost over, when a shot came from the one side of them, from a white cop in the rearguard. "Stop, you donders," shouted the cop jubilantly, as Induna went flying, his bag of mealies crashing to the ground.

Chops ran to Induna; Staffnurse, as quick as the shot itself, ran out and towards the policeman, the arms of his greatcoat spread wide, waving fiercely. "Donder, you donder yourself," he screamed at the cop, who hesitated for a moment. Then, as the coat was almost on him, the cop fired at it and scored a neat bull right through one of the most prominent patches. Missed the inhabitant, though; and before he could try another shot he was himself winged by Two Boy Sevenpence's Reserve Battalion.

Staffnurse rushed back to Induna, found him being helped through the fence by Chops, and the bag of mealies crawling after him. He bent down and picked up Lebane, and the four of them were through, and into Western Township.

Induna was bleeding, fast, and groaning sadly.

"Along here with him," said Lebane, "I can move along myself on this road." Staffnurse and Chops dragged and carried the big man along, while the squeal of castors came from the ground.

"Son," said Induna, "mustn't leave me near here. Mustn't have Congress tied up with this trouble."

"Won't leave you nowhere," said Staffnurse.

"I'm not going to last, boy, so you'll have to leave me somewhere soon," coughed Induna.

"We'll go to my place," said Lebane, "then we can say it's just another tsotsi-shooting. Plenty shooting there every night. Then we can take you to hospital."

"That's it," said Induna, with a tiny flash of his old twinkle, "blame the tsotsis."

They struggled on, through the rutted lanes of Western Township, over into Newclare and away towards Lebane's shantytown. Behind them the noises were dying down; the shootings and the yellings and the telegraph poles' song.

Staffnurse found an old wooden barrow inside a fence, quietly lifted it and they dumped both their invalids in it. Then they pushed at high speed. There were no curfew patrols to avoid that night, they were all out at Sophiatown.

They laid Induna down inside the Lebane's packing-case-and-sacking hut. Mrs. Lebane fetched clean water from the communal tap a hundred feet off, boiled it up and tried to stop Induna's bleeding. He was weak now.

"Staffnurse," he whispered, "afraid must've been

Dube started it all. Was police spy, Staffnurse, know that; said just working 'from within' police, was really Congress spy; don't believe it now, mascot. Think he started first trouble, Port Elizabeth."

"Yes, chief," said Staffnurse, "that Zenze he quite fine."

"Fine, Staff."

"Think he'll become our leader one day," said Staffnurse. He looked sad, his smile sunken away for ever. "But there'll never be another leader like you, chief."

"Will be another, Staff, good one, great one, he'll take the people out of this trouble we've made."

They didn't talk for a minute. The greatcoat patted the old shabby coat comfortingly.

"Staff," said the shabby coat softly, "education," he coughed painfully, paused, "maybe it'll be one like you."

20

LATTER DAYS

Morning. Very early, very frosty. A torn, aged patchwork greatcoat slithers and feels its way up a wide, concrete pipe. Date of greatcoat: Boer War, retired. Owner: Staffnurse Phofolo, also known as Jackson, also Mtetwa, who presently emerges, leaps on to the frosty ground, returns to whisper down the pipe. "Okay, Chops." Slithering and feeling a way out of the pipe follows Chops, discharged deliveryman, recently of Toby Street, Sophiatown.

The pipe was retracted into its pillbox, the hardware strewn about, the notice switched around and two military men went off into the city looking for jobs.

"Chops," said the greatcoat, "I'm getting better job. Going to educate more."

"Yah," said Chops. "That's what Induna said before he die. I'm going to also." He looked at this, found it very funny that he should give up the bicycle and tried out his uproarious laugh on it. Rustily, quietly at first, but soon its full, generous flush. "But watch out for the police for a couple days," he ended.

There were changes everywhere. The position of leader of Congress, now permanently underground, was one. Boniface Zenze beat the dark man on a vote, then felt that this new distinguished (even if underground) honour required the position of female consort to be filled, too. Vacancy advertised, application made by a Miss S. Nkomo. Application approved and accepted. Among presents received was fat dictionary, lovingly inscribed "from a former regular customer, S. Phofolo." Left further vacancy in heart of same former customer. As yet unfilled.

Leadership and very many positions of trust also open in several Sophiatown "committees" and "protection services", due to active service casualties. Amalgamations between Moonlights and Pretty Boys; between Torch Commando and Shiners, solved most problems. Later, disagreement over territory between those two sets resulted in further casualties, one very small gang remaining. Leader: Two Boy Sevenpence. Changed his name to Two Boy One-and-Sevenpence.

By the time the Parliament sits again, nearly everyone has forgotten the riots, except the methodical Mnr. Kob who brings his Bill up for an amendment, to take care of such circumstances in the future. It is necessary to add just one clause.

And Professor Hampshire, who warns the House that

this sort of trouble will become much rougher, as this sort of Bill gets tougher. "Next time," he says, "it will be more than a riot; a revolt."

Parpenfus is cycling eagerly over to him in the Lobby, to see what he intends to do next; but he's a puzzled man, he hardly knows.

"A lunch," thinks Hampshire dreamily, "that's it, a lunch. Pancakes in rum," he licks his lips.

The Lobby drifts on, the House drifts on; Pumpernickel nods and naps, the public gape, Mevrou Futsheim preens her bottom, the public gapes harder, Bargoyle worries about his money matters, the public worries about its. Outside, ten million blacks dance away on the point of a needle. It's all for the best in the best of all possible worlds.